The Napper

The Napper

Linh Luu

EPONYMOUS
BOOKS

The Napper

For public appearances contact:

www.eponymousbooks.com

ISBN NO: 9798894122878

EPONYMOUS
BOOKS

Linh Luu

For my younger self and all the young women before me who ever had a big dream that took them across the world and back.

The Napper

Linh Luu

"*Each time she started reading a book she liked, she would fill with fear, shame, and endless sadness because this good book was whole, and the thing that was Anna's book would not become whole, would never become one with the world, one with these books and their wholeness, and because Anna was not whole, could never be so, could never become this person who was one with the world and sure of their place in it.*"

- MY WORK *by Olga Ravn*

ix

The Napper

The Napper

Chapter One

September 2014, Chapel Hill

When you were fourteen and told your parents that you wanted to go to the U.S. for boarding school, they decided to believe you, because they wanted a daughter who could make the family look good through academic achievement. This validation was what you said you wanted to give them. Now five years later, you are in college, and know in your heart that you will never return to Hanoi.

The long days of summer had passed. The days were getting shorter and cooler. I started unpacking my bags, and put up a poster of Adele that I had from my boarding school days. I saw that the right side of my room, where my roommate Sooji would sleep, was already all set up. She had neatly organized her toiletries and stationary by color and size. For me, the need to arrange one's room felt like a burden. I threw the stuff from my suitcases onto the bed. I hated unpacking just like I hated doing any domestic labor.

At home, there was always someone around to help—my maid, my driver, a cousin. In boarding school, I'd had to wear a blazer and some kind of button-down shirt; here I didn't have a clue about what I should be wearing. I had a UNC tee shirt and a gray UNC sweatshirt. I felt like Hermione Granger suddenly stripped of the Hogwarts uniform she'd worn her whole adolescence. I looked in the mirror and thought, "You're an eighteen-year-old woman and you're wearing sweatpants and a sweatshirt."

I had gained twenty pounds during the last two years of high school, all of which seemed to have gone to my thighs and arms. My belly remained flat which amazed me, but my thighs chafed when I walked, and my ass, which had previously looked pleasingly curvy, now felt like a burden. This was something my mother did not hesitate to point out and criticize every time she saw me during the previous summer in Hanoi. My non-existent A-cup boobs on the other hand had barely grown. The result was that they looked like two drooping lemons. I couldn't shake a perpetual sense of physical inadequacy. I found it preferable to be ignored than to be noticed. Blending into the shadows was a defense mechanism that I had learned from boarding school. Besides, it seemed people had always ignored me, and I didn't see the need to try to change that.

I had my first emotional breakdown my last semester of high school, right after I'd been accepted to Yale. My ultimate academic achievement at the time didn't equate to a sensation of euphoria like I had convinced myself all those years. I still felt as small and inconsequential as I did when I first arrived to America. Yet, the people at my prestigious boarding school in Pennsylvania saw me as this academic wiz. Pretending to be one the last four years had stifled my authentic self, and I felt like something had died inside me. To dull the high emotional intensity of my unhappiness, I began to take long naps at random hours, every single day. If napping were a sport, I'd be a world champion. Napping was the only time I felt relief from the guilt and shame of being a fraud. Napping, I could regularly relax into the truest state of consciousness, one without form. I had achieved something tangible that could make my status-conscious parents happy, and napping was how I rewarded myself for years of academic labor. As soon as a nap ended, I'd find myself in the next state, the natural consequence of waking: hyper-anxiety. Anxiety was an old friend. To the world I showed a brave face, forcing myself to laugh at other people's jokes, make small talk and perform social niceties. But inside, I felt like a perpetual fish out of water.

The Napper

I had been offered a small scholarship to Yale and my parents could afford to pay the rest of the tuition. But instead, I decided to "prove myself" by accepting a rare merit-based scholarship to UNC. It already felt like a mistake. The moment I walked onto the campus and saw the uniformly gray dormitories, not unlike the communist buildings in Vietnam, I felt the urge to throw up. I'd had mixed feelings about going to college but when I got the scholarship letter in the mail, I resigned myself to its inevitability. The alternative, which I'd briefly considered, was to stay in Hanoi and marry the son of one of my parents' acquaintances. When my auntie introduced me to a high-ranking cop, the son of the Premier of Hanoi, it helped me make up my mind. He talked to me as if I were an exotic bird who had flown away to America and then returned to its rightful place. I may have sometimes felt at odds in the academic settings of the U.S., but I was decidedly not cut out for the life of a domestic wife in Vietnam.

Sooji looked like an Asian Barbie. She wore a white tennis skirt, off-white sneakers, and a cropped Tommy Hilfiger bra. She had long, slightly wavy hair, the kind of style that you needed specific hair tools to achieve. It was called mermaid hair or something like that. When we had messaged over the summer, I'd learned that Sooji was Korean-American, and that she was from the Bay Area. Her parents worked in Silicon

Valley. For some reason, in boarding school, I'd had white or black roommates, never anybody of Asian descent. Having Sooji as my roommate felt like a breath of fresh air. She walked in just as I was stirring from my nap. She had a couple of large canvas bags with her. They made a thud when she dropped them to the ground.

"Hi there! You're finally here! It's *Thigh* right?"

"Um, no. Actually, it's Thuy, pronounced like Tweety Bird."

"Oh silly me," she said, her smile revealing prominent canine teeth that made me think of a cute vampire. "I'm Sooji."

Sooji started unpacking her canvas bags. The items she proceeded to reveal included a blender, a seltzer maker, a glorious Nespresso machine, and Nespresso pods. I didn't think I would be excited to live in a dormitory, but seeing how she was accessorizing the place I couldn't help but be elated.

"Did you do anything fun over the summer?" I asked her.

"I was mostly home, except for going scuba diving in Barbados for a week and then a short stop in Palm Beach. What about you?" she asked.

"Oh, just spending time with my family in Hanoi."

"Woah, what's Hanoi like? I've always wanted to go."

"It's a lovely place, for sure." I showed her some pictures of my family's vacation to Hoi An and Nha Trang. I didn't know if she could tell that my smile was forced in all of the photos, even when they were photos of us at five-star resorts overlooking the pristine Southeast Asia Sea. I showed her a picture of my younger brother, my mother, and me sitting in the lobby of a posh resort. My mom was stylishly dressed, with perfectly applied makeup and shiny black hair that went all the way to her backside. I was used to people going on about how beautiful and young she looked. Out of obligation, I too felt compelled to feed her compliments, even if the favor was rarely returned.

"Aw, your family looks so cute! And your mom, wow, she looks very young!"

"Thanks," I said. Every time I thought about my mom, a wave of melancholy ran over me. It reminded me of the reason why I'd left home in the first place. Sooji asked if I'd like to join her and her parents for dinner that night.

"Sure," I replied. I was curious to see what their family dynamic was like.

The first orientation event was in a big auditorium. I picked a random seat next to a guy who wore a t-shirt with the UNC mascot. The caricature of the ram looked a bit stupid and juvenile, and I wondered why college was so much like kindergarten. I was proud of having been educated during my early years in the French education system in Hanoi where there was zero bullshit infantilization. Because of it, I felt oddly comfortable being in a space where I knew nobody, and nobody knew me. I felt that if I wanted to, I could disappear and no one would notice. Thus, I was resigned to the idea of getting by not making any friends. Though I did like Sooji.

The first part on the orientation program was organized by the student's association. It was a performance of students doing different activities: going to class, to the dining hall, the gym. I couldn't figure out the point of the performance except that perhaps it was a time-killer before the next speaker, the Dean of Students. He gave a speech about the school's values. Lux and Libertas. He repeated things we already knew from the brochures and incessant emails. That this was one of the best research universities in the world yada, yada. After the dean's speech, which went in one ear and out the other, I figured I should at least try to make a friend. I turned to the guy next to me and asked him why he had chosen to come to UNC.

"Duke rejected me," he said.

I tried to smile politely.

Later, I walked around the campus with a smaller group. There was a generic looking tall white guy with curly blonde hair, a petite black girl wearing a red A-line dress, a nerdy Asian guy wearing a sports jersey, and a couple more kids who for some reason I could tell were definitely from North Carolina. At the undergraduate library, our guide said: "You guys will most likely be spending the majority of your time here." The building was painted a dreary dark grey, and looked like two humongous cement blocks stacked atop each other. The word that came to mind was Chernobyl.

On the other side of campus was the newer "graduate" library. It was seven stories tall and reminded me of a corporate structure. In between the two libraries was the bookstore. A group of hipsters were sitting on the steps out front, some reading, some chatting. On the square in front of the bookstore were some skateboarders doing tricks.

A boy dribbling a basketball shouted, "This is the UNC way." I would soon find out that for some, the UNC basketball team was like a religion. There was a lottery system for students to get tickets. For the most coveted Duke versus UNC games, many students camped outside of the stadium just to put their names in.

"Hey," I said to the black girl, trying to make small talk. "The campus looks nice enough."

She feigned a smile. The guide kept on talking as he walked us to the other side of the quad. The girl,

Ines, according to her name tag, turned to me and said, "Yes. This is a beautiful campus, built entirely by black slaves." I looked at her and felt relief that someone was as cynical about it all as myself.

"Look it up," she said. "Hundreds of enslaved people were forced to build it in the 1700s. And they didn't let the first Black student in until 1951."

I didn't know what to say in response so I nodded and made a little grunt of agreement. I felt annoyed at myself for what seemed like a preternatural inability to make small talk. In boarding school, I'd used my awkwardness for my own benefit: I stayed in rather than socialized at events, and my grade point average thrived. Yet I'd also felt tremendously isolated. I had since decided to make small talk in the hopes of tricking some other souls into some kind of camaraderie. The last time I'd felt any kind of connection with my classmates was back in Vietnam in 9th grade. For all my ambivalence about how being social might impact my academic life, I was sick of feeling so alienated.

At lunch, in the cold floor of the cafeteria, I stood in line, waiting to sample the food I'd be consuming for the next four years. I'd been looking forward to experiencing true Southern cuisine. What I got was mealy chicken fingers, "al dente" mac and cheese, soggy collard greens, and lukewarm pizza. I attempted to make conversation a second time with

Ines. She was the only person in the cohort that I had any inkling of a desire to befriend. For starters, she had a name that could be Moroccan, and I was curious to see if we had any common French schooling in our background. But before I could ask her, she was already asking me where I was from. "Before this, I went to The Hill School in Pennsylvania, however I'm originally from Vietnam. Hanoi."

"Wait, are you also in the scholarship program? I think I saw your face in the student directory."

"Oh yeah. So are you also–?"

"Yep," she said.

Her brown skin contrasted beautifully with her raspberry red dress. I once again felt ashamed of my sweatsuit.

"What about you? Are you from here?"

"Nope," she said. "I'm from South Africa."

"I've never been to Africa. I'd really like to go, though."

"Well—I've been to Hanoi. I went to school in Singapore," she said. If the rest of the cohort of the people I went on the tour with had American names like Jake and Lizzy, meeting Ines felt like a breath of fresh air. My insecurity about meeting new people dissipated slightly. I'd already connected with Ines and Sooji on my first day. Maybe it wouldn't be so bad after all.

When I got back to my room, Sooji wasn't there. I sat at my desk and looked out the window. We were on the 7th floor of a red-brick building, and our view was of the southside of campus. There were rolling hills and other dorms, taller than ours. Checking my WhatsApp, I saw that there were no new texts. I wanted to call Mom, but it was 4 am in Vietnam. Earlier in the day, she had sent a nice text. "Happy first day of school. Love you." Mom and I had had a big fight before I had left, so her message seemed forced. At dinner a week before I left, she accused me of having changed, of having become too American because I bit into an apple rather than slicing it and offering pieces to other family members at the table. She stood over me, glowering and rattling off a litany of the ways I had changed. Her words came at me rapid fire, like little bullets of negativity. I sat placidly and took it. When she got like this, I rarely responded. But deep down, I felt a simmering anger.

Sooji invited me to join her and her parents at a Mexican place.

"So what are you studying Thuy?" Steve, Sooji's father, asked. His gray hair stuck out from the sides of his baseball cap. Sooji's mom, Nina, was skinny, and her face reminded me of the kind of mom I wished I had: one with whom I could chitchat, perhaps even share secrets with. Not one whose validation and attention I desperately craved.

"I'm not declared yet. But I think English Literature," I said.

"That's exciting," Steve said, sipping his Dr. Pepper.

"Sooji's thinking of doing anthropology, aren't you?" Nina said.

Sooji mumbled, "Yeah."

The waiters brought chips and guacamole and then tacos. It always surprised me how many different foods I had yet to try.

"We don't have a lot of tacos shops in Hanoi," I said.

"We bring Sooji to Asia once a year," Nina said, "and we've been to Saigon, but not yet Hanoi."

"My father was in the Vietnam War," Steve said. When it seemed that he remembered that my dad was from Hanoi, and that his father was probably trying to kill my father, he quickly added, "I can't imagine how much the country must have changed since then."

"You have to come and visit us one day," Nina said, changing the subject. "Yeah, Thuy, if you don't already have plans, come for Thanksgiving! You can stay with us," Sooji said.

"Thank you," I said with sincere gratitude.

Back in the dorm, I felt grateful to have been matched with Sooji. I'd been afraid that the fates would have me paired with a harsh and aggressive roommate. Yet they had been kind. Sooji was funny and convivial and she inexplicably seemed to like me.

The next morning, Sooji woke up early and went on her run. Meanwhile, I stayed in bed and looked at my phone. Just the buzz of social media. Nothing new there. Then, even though I had only been awake for an hour, I decided to take a nap. The result was that I was late for my first English lecture. When I entered the classroom, the professor was talking about the marriage plot in Jane Austen's *Pride and Prejudice*. Donning my invisibility cloak, I sat down in the back and started to take notes in longhand. After ten minutes, my mind began to wander. It was all I could do to not fold my arms into a little pillow and lay down my head. My thoughts wandered to why I had come to this little town in North Carolina in the first place. Such a strange confluence of events. But, deep down, I knew it was my ambition that had brought me there. To make a name for myself and set myself apart from the upper-class bubble I'd grown up in. For as much as I loved my homeland, I wanted to be the next Marguerite Duras.

At lunch in the cafeteria, I ate ravioli and a mixed green salad. Chewing on its chewy texture made me miss the food from home: pho, rice with real chicken and soup, fish, actual not overcooked vegetables. Even though I had spent most of the last few years in America, I had never gotten used to starchy, glutinous cafeteria food. I supplemented it with junk food. Hence my oversized figure. While mechanically chewing the ravioli, I read Flaubert's *Sentimental Education.* I enjoyed this novel quite a lot, but nevertheless, I began skimming midway through, eager to reach the ending. I was always eager to get to the end of things. I was also eager to get to the end of this tasteless meal. To get through being a perpetual student and go out and experience life for real, like Frederic Moreau.

All of the scholarship kids were due to meet that evening at John Hall for a banquet type dinner where the head of the scholarship association would give a speech, followed by a speech by an alumnus of the program. I decided to wear a black silk slip dress with red strappy heels. I texted Ines to ask if she wanted to go together. She responded with a happy face emoji. When she saw me in front of the dorm, she did a double take and said, "You clean up well!"

"Thanks," I said, feeling self-conscious. I had only worn this dress once before, in Hanoi, and my mother had made a disparaging comment. "How was your first day of classes?" she asked me.

"Not as remarkable as I'd hoped," I said. "It's hard for me to relate to Elizabeth Bennet."

"Who?"

"The protagonist of *Pride and Prejudice.*"

She laughed. "I know what you mean."

Fidgety students were gathered around round, white tablecloth covered tables in the crowded banquet room. Most of the seats were already taken when we got there, and we separated to find our assigned seats. I noticed a boy who came in late, after the talk had begun. How could I not notice? His skin was sard-brown. He had short curls and was extremely tall, all muscle and no fat. His blazer and dress pants looked a bit oversized, and perhaps vintage. He sat down next to me, turned to me, and smiled. He wore glasses and when he looked at me, his eyes had the effect of a warm bright light. He had a welcoming presence. His name tag said, "Oscar." I'd never met anyone with this name before, and I thought it sounded very American.

At the podium, the guest speaker, who had invented a DNA testing website, talked about the privilege of being part of a community of scholars, and encouraged us to take advantage of the opportunities that would come from this experience.

"What do you major in, Oscar?" I asked. I had noticed that the name tag on his shirt indicated that he was a senior. I did the math. He was probably three years older than me.

"Computer science and finance," he replied.

"Cool."

"What about you?"

"I think Art History, but I haven't declared it yet. It's funny because I came in thinking I would study English lit but I changed my mind."

"What changed your mind?"

"I want to study the language of art." I left it at that, and he looked somewhat bemused by my cryptic answer.

The waiters brought us our dinner. Chicken au poivre.

I then started a conversation with the woman seated on the other side of me, a professor of Classics. She was Haitian-American, she told me in an elegant accent. She had long braids that framed her oval face and opal blue eyes. I told her that I'd taken four years of Greek and Latin but didn't feel as confident as I should. After all, how often was I able to put these languages to use? When I first arrived in the States, I used to feel like Odysseus lost at sea, but I later realized, with a painful feeling of shame, that the reverse was true. Whenever I returned to Hanoi, I felt like I was cast away, and despite the familiar food and people, I could feel myself itching to leave. For me, home would never be an easy concept.

Oscar took advantage of a break in the conversation to ask me, "Were you the girl reading *Sentimental Education* in the cafeteria?"

"Well, yes," I said.

"Hmm," he said, as if making a mental note.

"Why? Have you read it before?"

"Well, yes," he said. "A teacher in my lycée days back in Senegal gave it as a reading assignment."

"No way. *Tu parles Français?*"

"*Oui.*" And then we switched to talking in French.

"*J'ai grandi au Sénégal puis j'ai déménagé à New York à l'âge de quinze ans,*" he said.

"*Ah ouais? Moi j'suis arrive ici quand j'ai quinze ans aussi, de Vietnam.*" I replied. I wanted to ask him more questions, but just then, the dean came on the microphone announcing another guest speaker.

After the dinner, we exchanged phone numbers.

"Keep me updated on what you're reading," he said. "I feel like I'll need your cultural expertise as I sink deeper and deeper into coding."

Back at the dorm, Sooji asked me about the banquet. I told her it had been an eventful dinner.

"Really?" she said playfully. "Or are you being sarcastic?"

"It was fine."

"Are you planning to sign up for any clubs?" she asked me.

"I don't think so," I said. She looked a bit confused, and I was worried she'd think that I didn't have a life. The truth was, I wanted to try out my new experiment: seeing how little I could do and still get by. I didn't think anybody else would care. After all, my family was halfway around the world. And this was an Art History degree. I felt like I could probably just sleepwalk and stay unencumbered.

I wanted to tell her about Oscar. Did I like him? But I just said goodnight and went straight to bed. I was anxiously anticipating the next morning, where there would be a check for fifteen thousand dollars waiting for me at the Bursar's office. I hoped.

The thing that made living in North Carolina tolerable was time. I had quite a lot of it. To get the scholarship, I'd had to sweat and struggle, but now, I could ease up. Ease way up. I felt the desire to nap whenever I had an inkling to. Instead of signing up for the most intense courses, I picked the lightest load. Most of my classes were scheduled for the morning. I'd wake. Look at my phone, go back to sleep, get up, throw on some sweats, go to my one class (out of the three classes I signed up for), get a Chick-fil-A sandwich at the cafeteria and return to my dorm. Eat that and have another nap. Fuck it. I was proud of my ability to nap at will–my body needed to detox from the built-up stress in my life.

One day, in maybe the third week of school, I woke up from my nap to find Sooji in the room. She wore a cute jersey and a pink skirt. I was in my usual attire, gray sweats. She was sitting at her desk, painting her toenails a bright pink.

"No practice today?" I asked, hoping that I didn't sound annoyed.

"No, it was canceled," she said. "What about you? Still no activities?"

"Nope," I said. "I just go to class and then come home."

She raised her eyebrows, pursed her lips, and then smiled. As if she'd just gotten a brilliant idea.

"We should go to the Arboretum together. Before you can protest, I will even buy you frozen yogurt. I feel bad that we never hang together as roommates."

I couldn't come up with a good excuse off the top of my head, so I agreed.

Sitting on the green grass, smelling the yellow dandelions and violets (if North Carolinians can be proud of anything, it's their gardens), my skin felt warm from the sunshine. I wasn't used to it. It's not that I tried to avoid the outdoors, it just didn't fit into my lifestyle.

"So, what's new these days?" Sooji asked me.

"Not much," I replied. I switched my position, lying down on the ground.

Sooji followed suit.

"How are your parents?" I asked her, attempting to be social.

"They're good--you know, my mom asked about you the other day. I told her that you were doing fine, even though we haven't had a chance to catch up."

I tried to smile politely. I liked Sooji, and her parents were nice. And, rather than keeping mum like

I usually would, suddenly, I decided to open up. "Not going to lie," I said. "I feel like I have zero direction in my life. I feel like one of those floaties with nothing tethering me to Earth. I called my parents the other day, and I held back tears. From what? I don't even know." I worried I had totally turned off Sooji by divulging my whole torrent of emotions.

"I see where you're coming from. When I was fifteen, we had this girl we hosted from China. She was pretty and smart but every night I could hear her crying in her bedroom. I didn't want to embarrass her, so I never brought it up. But it always made me feel bad, knowing that she felt alone and lonely. When I saw you in your bed in the middle of the day for the third time in a row, it reminded me of her. Back then, I was not as emotionally mature as I am now, so I ignored her. I just don't want you to feel like I'm ignoring you."

Before I could repress the tears, they started falling down.

Sooji moved over to me and held my hand while I wept. I could tell that we were disturbing the group of quiet picnickers and students attempting to study nearby.

When I finally composed myself, I wiped my eyes and nose and my fingers on my tote bag. I smiled and shrugged my shoulders. Sooji said gently, "Come on now. Let's go get some froyo." We got up and walked to the frozen yogurt place. Sooji put her arm around me as we waited in line.

Chapter Two

A week later - Chapel Hill

I was on my way to French class. The trees were brightly lit, and the leaves made me think of a colony of fat starfish. I did not realize how steep the hill between my dorm and the class would be, and so I was a bit winded when I entered the classroom. Much to my surprise, Oscar was sitting in the front row. I immediately felt happy, seeing him. I was excited at the prospect of becoming his friend. Something about his thick black glasses reminded me of Malcolm X. He wore a tee shirt that said "Amoeba Records," jeans, and red Air Jordans. His long, skinny limbs barely fit under the desk. I picked a seat next to him.

"Hey there," I said, trying to sound nonchalant. I didn't want to reveal too much. But I felt that being friends with someone who came from a similar background would be helpful. I needed help getting through North Carolina. Not that Vietnam and Senegal were anything close to the same, as far as I knew. But, bottom line, I wanted him to like me.

"Hmm," he said. His eyes remained focused on a giant Calculus textbook he was reading. I was a little annoyed that he didn't reciprocate conversation, but I figured he might just be studious. At that point, class finally started.

The teacher, Professor Roberts, had written down some keywords about Madame Bovary.

Ennui

Le Realisme

Professor Roberts was a stocky woman with short hair. She was wearing an olive green shirt dress, and she smelled like lilies, the scent of which somehow emanated all the way to where I sat.

"Hello class, I will soon begin speaking in French, and I expect our class conversation to remain in French, as this is Advanced Level French. If you have any concerns or would like to be placed in a different section, feel free to reach out to me later."

Now introducing herself in French, she said, "My name is Louisa, and I am your French teacher. I was born and raised in Boston. I graduated from Harvard in 2010 with a PhD in French Literature. My research was on Foucault's early years and mental illness. In my free time, I like to walk my two sausage dogs,

Beckett and Durkheim, around town, and to bake cookies. Now please go around the room and introduce yourself."

I always struggled with remembering my classmates names and faces. There were only seven of us, and they were all white Americans except for me and Oscar.

"Hello everyone. My name is Oscar. I was born and raised in Dakar, Senegal and then moved to the U.S. when I was fifteen. I intend to major in Computer Science. My favorite things to do are to play basketball and to study science. Oh, and I have a cat named Millie." His voice was deep in a way that could only be described as philosophical. I'd honestly never heard a voice so calm and resonant before.

Louisa asked him if he was on the school's basketball team. I could see the other students' ears perk up. For the last few days, all the students had been talking about getting tickets to the UNC-Duke game, even though basketball season wouldn't even start until November.

"Nope. I plan on trying out for the JV team though. I had been trying the past few years but had yet to be recruited."

"Exciting! Please let the class know when you do."

I had always felt slightly jealous of school athletes. What did it feel like to devote yourself, your *body* so selflessly to a common goal? My only goal now was to not participate, which sometimes felt like a sport in its own right. Like I said. If napping was an Olympic sport, I'd definitely be the gold medalist. When it was my turn, I told the class, "My name is Thuy. I'm from Hanoi, Vietnam, but I moved to the U.S. at fifteen. Art History major. On the weekends, I like to just relax."

"Very good. We all need to relax more," Professor R said.

"Not me," Oscar said under his breath.

"And why is that Oscar?"

"If I relax, I can't get anything done."

I felt a bit annoyed by his little comment but decided to keep quiet. High achievers generally annoyed me. From my own experience, too much work only led to ennui. Then again, I used to be a high achiever, not too long ago. In boarding school, I used to stay up till 2am to get through SAT prep, after finishing my work as editor of the school newspaper and for the student philanthropy council, and all my AP-class homework. All that work ultimately led to me hating my life. My new experiment. Doing the least, except what I wanted to do. That was my new motto. People weren't my forte, I told myself. If only it was as easy to make friends as it was to nap.

Returning to the class main topic, Professor R told us that we would start off with *Madame Bovary.*

"*Madame Bovary,* written in 1856 by Gustave Flaubert, is about a bored housewife who resides in the countryside and chooses to commit adultery in order to escape her sense of loss and *ennui*. Can anybody guess which other novel Flaubert based his portrayal of Madame Bovary on? Without skipping a beat, both Oscar and I said, *"Don Quixote."* Oscar looked at me and smiled. He seemed impressed.

I had been obsessed with the play version of *Don Quixote* since I had acted in it in French school in Hanoi. I played Dulcinea, the princess that Don Quixote falls in love with, because to him, she represents an ideal, the source of all inspiration and faith. Of course, she'd reject him in the end, even after he completes the tasks that she asks of him. I had once been Don Quixote, excitedly packing my bags for the U.S., thinking that a better future awaited me. I couldn't have known then that four years later, I'd end up a young ball of bitterness, resenting people—friends, family, professors-anyone or anything that infringed on my time. On my project. The napping project was the only thing that brought me happiness. But with Oscar, I was tempted to get interested, to get distracted.

When I got back to the dorm that afternoon, I tried to get started on my homework, but before even finishing twenty pages of *Madame Bovary*, I felt incapable of continuing. I felt a sense of tightness in my chest.

At boarding school, I could sublimate my emotions by studying day and night. But the freedom that college afforded opened up new avenues of disquietude. I'd had no difficulty working constantly in high school. I got good grades, I came close to being valedictorian, I got my scholarship. My goals were manifested…and yet. Why did everything feel so overwhelming? A ghost from the past seemed to be after me. It felt to me like I'd tried to escape my childhood and Hanoi, but it was all catching up with me. My eyes wanted to close. I told myself I needed to stay awake at least one more hour until the acceptable time of eight pm. I looked around the room and tried to readjust my body. Feeling dead inside, I walked over to my bed and got under the warm green comforter. I was still wearing my clothes, a dirty white sweatshirt and black polyester pants. I didn't understand why I felt so tired all the time. For now, I'd go back to bed and let sleep take care of everything.

The next morning, when I woke up, I looked at the clock. 7 am. I'd been asleep a hearty eleven hours. The morning nap was another hour. Twelve hours! Every day I seemed to be exceeding my previous capacity for slumbering. That I was proud of something that most people saw as indulgent gave me a jolt of pleasure. Napping was like eating one too many chocolate cookies, but better, because you didn't get chubbier.

The Napper

Sooji was still in her bed, sleeping. I could hear her breathing from my side of the room. I went over to the Nespresso and picked out my favorite pod, Ristretto, and put it in the machine. Funny enough, even though the Nespresso was Sooji's, she rarely drank it because she had to leave so early for volleyball practice. She did, however, make me my first ever Espresso Martini. It tasted so strong that I felt like throwing up, but I tried to act cool and pretend to like it.

After the espresso, I decided to go for a walk to clear my head. I put on my sneakers and looked at my phone. Sooji had messaged me yesterday evening asking if I wanted to go to a party with her. Good thing I'd missed that. I hated social situations where I didn't know the people around me. Like orientation day, when I'd tried to suck up to the people there. I feared people wouldn't find me likable, and that I was bound to say something stupid. Sometimes, during an event or party, I'd have the chilling fantasy that someone, a supposed friend, would come up and remove the mask from my face. Once unmasked, the real me would be revealed. The me that was disgusting, to be shunned by all those around me.

The path leading from the dorm was surrounded on each side by grass. There were some yellow daffodils and jacarandas. I smelled the clean scent of the morning air, different from the thick smoke of Hanoi. Even though I'd lived in the U.S. for four years now, I still compared everything to back home. Yes, it was cleaner here, but I craved the fumes and smog of the streets of Hanoi. I had no clear direction as I kept walking. I walked up the hill and then down the other side, following the flow of traffic towards the town of Chapel Hill. There were early risers on their morning run and students strolling. I walked past beautiful white and light-yellow homes, the post office, a CVS, and several restaurants not yet open. Suddenly, the aroma of sausages and eggs came wafting from the open door of a restaurant. The place was named "Egg Yolk."

I entered and took a seat at the breakfast bar. The place was small, and the bar stools were covered in red leather. There were a few customers at the tables in the back, but only me and a middle aged man sat at the breakfast counter. He had on a hoodie and was ostensibly listening to music on his headphones as he typing what looked like a long string of numbers on his laptop.

The waitress walked over to me. She was tall, with large hazel eyes, short brown hair, and a friendly demeanor. I asked for coffee, cream and sugar. She nodded and wrote it down on a little notepad. "Also blueberry ricotta pancakes please. Oh, and a side of bacon."

"You must be hungry," a voice said. It was Oscar. He sat down on the stool next to mine.

"Oh - hi!"

He smiled at me, which was weird, because he hadn't even looked at me when we were leaving French class yesterday.

"How it's going?" I asked him.

"Good, just working on my compsci stuff."

"I grew up completely blind and unaware of how technology works, so to me that seems very impressive."

"It's not that hard," he replied.

The waitress took his order, and then he explained to me more about what he was studying. It all sounded like mumbo jumbo to me. Still, I liked the tone and timbre of his voice. It was relaxing.

The waitress brought over my pancakes and a salad for Oscar.

"Are you eating salad for breakfast?" "Don't look so shocked," he said.

"Don't tell me you're a vegan," I joked.

Seeing the awkward look on his face, I immediately regretted what I'd said, but it was too late. I'd been a vegan for a few hours once, but then I'd succumbed to my mother's cooking. It was almost impossible to be vegan when you're surrounded by spring rolls, vermicelli with pork, and beef *pho*.

"Yeah. I'm a vegan."

I couldn't help myself and started laughing. It was so like me to say something without thinking and then offend someone.

"How are you liking Madame Bovary?" he asked in an attempt to change the subject.

"Well, I haven't gotten around to re-reading it," I said. "However, when I first read it, I loved everything about it. Yesterday, when I was trying to read it, I fell asleep at eight and didn't wake up until seven a.m. this morning."

"Are you okay?"

I nodded. "It's probably just jet lag," I said, knowing full well that my flight from Vietnam had been a few days ago, and it wasn't jetlag.

There was a bit of silence before I asked him, "Do you ever do anything BESIDES working?"

"Yes. I mean, I play intramural basketball. But no, not much else."

"That's fascinating," I said, trying not to sound bored.

"I want to try doing the things that kids in college do, like going out and meeting people," I said. I took a big bite of pancake. With a full mouth, I blurted out, "You're my friend!"

He smiled at me. "Yes, friend. We're now breakfast buddies."

"Breakfast buddies," I said, thinking that Oscar was just as nerdy as I was.

But I was a nerd who wasn't doing all of her reading. Did that un-nerd me?

I wondered what it would be like to have close friends in college. Sure, I had Sooji, but we weren't as close as I'd have liked. There seemed to always be an invisible barrier between us. I'd never had super close female friends.

With Oscar though, I felt safe, which was strange, considering we'd just met.

***

Hanoi, 2003

I'm scared to leave my room. Mom is there. Last night she shouted at me and said that she didn't want me in the living room, disturbing her peace. I can hear her voice talking on the phone to a client, making sales. Her job is very important to her. She works for a large pharmaceutical company in Hanoi. Her boss is a huge bully and makes her do all of the work. So yesterday, when I went out to the living room, she yelled at me. She yells at all of us when the table isn't set right. She'll say things like that our maid, Tina, had cooked us a perfectly decent meal but the useless members of her family were incompetent when it came to placing bowls and plates where they should be. She yells that the soup bowl is placed too far to the left, the meat to the right, and the rice not quite close enough to the center of the table. And then she'll yell at my father. "You're a useless tool! I make all the decisions at work and then I have to come home to teach you how to set plates correctly!" A lot of worse things are said after that. Like how she has to help everybody in the family and nobody helps her in return. Yesterday, I felt both angry at her for yelling and guilty. And yet, she's right. Without her, we wouldn't be living in our dream home - a beautiful penthouse in the center of Hanoi. My little brother and I wouldn't be able to go to the international French school. She grew up dirt poor, the youngest of ten children in rural Vietnam, so I know she had to fight tooth and nail to be where she is today. I can't imagine what she had to go through…and I know there are things that she went through that destroyed her spirit.

Anyway, why am I writing about this when it's a beautiful Sunday morning and nobody has done anything to me? I should be grateful that I get to wake up in a nice home with a meal waiting for me in the kitchen. I am craving Banh Mi with lots of ham, pickled cucumber and carrot. I can't wait to stay home and do nothing but watch MTV all day.

Chapter Three

A couple of weeks later, Chapel Hill

"Wake up, Thuy! It's already 9:30. Don't you have French at 8:45?" I heard Sooji's voice. But my shoulders ached. In fact, my whole body was aching. How long had I been sleeping in this strange position? My face plopped on the bed, my arms pinned down by my own body.

"Oh shit. I'm so late."

Sooji was in her tennis clothes, holding two cappuccinos in clear glass mugs. "I don't think it's worth it to even go now," I said, sitting up in my itty-bitty twin-size bed, trying to remember what had happened in the last twenty four hours. I remembered coming back to the dorm after my Latin class and then starting to type on my laptop. What had I been working on? Oh, yes. My grant. I needed the grant because I wanted to escape Chapel Hill. If I got the grant, then I'd get to spend the summer in Paris and leave this onehorse town. It was only four weeks into the school year, but I was already itching to leave.

"It's okay, I mean it's not like you skip classes often." Sooji held out a mug to me.

"Thanks, Sooj," I said. "I'm going to have to ask Oscar for notes." I imagined Oscar, the workaholic, raising an eyebrow when he heard about my strange sleeping schedule.

"Who?"

Sooji put on lip balm, then brushed her hair into a ponytail. Her face in the mirror looked like a model's. She was a model young woman, somebody who took care of herself. I wondered what I looked like to the world. My frizzy hair was always a bit tangled from sleeping all the time (and perhaps from not trying hard to make it look decent).

"Oscar is this guy in my French class. He's also a scholarship kid, so we met on the first day of orientation."

"So he's smart *and* he speaks French? Could this be a romantic connection, I wonder?"

I laughed and feeling embarrassed, said, "I don't think so. But I sure hope that he gives me the notes I need for French."

Sooji said something like she was hoping to date as many good-looking athletic guys as possible in the next couple of months.

"Well, you know what they say," she continued. "Half of the point of college is finding your dream partner. So, we can break it down into a timeline. Freshman year: date as much as possible. Sophomore year: Try out your first boyfriend for size. Hopefully, there's time to find another if the first one doesn't work out. Junior year: Lock him down. Senior year: get engaged," Sooji said with conviction.

I took a sip of my coffee. Sooji was the most strategic person I'd ever met. I found her logic outrageous. I could barely get myself to do the bare minimum in class, let alone meet a guy. Sooji's plans wouldn't work with girls like me.

"Why do you want to find your husband here of all places?" I asked, feeling like I wouldn't want to mate somewhere where the highest tier of social hierarchy were people in frats.

"Think about it Thuy, where else are there going to be so many candidates in the same place!"

"I'll never get married," I mumbled. "Getting married means being tied down, and why would you want that?"

"Well, that's your thinking. I think marriage is beautiful. And what about LOVE?"

"Love?" I chuckled. I didn't have time for love.

The undergraduate library was a squat, two-story building whose exterior reminded me of the communist government buildings in Hanoi. The interior had a more elegant, less brutalist feel. There weren't too many students at the library mid-day. I sat at a gorgeous, art deco wood table and jotted down what I wanted to research that summer. Maybe the influence of the French on Vietnamese art in the early 20th century. After doing a quick Google search, I found out that when the French were colonizing Vietnam, they established a school called École des Beaux-Arts in Hanoi. They sent a French painter named Victor Tardieu to teach the next generation of Vietnamese painters. In my research, I saw many embroidered "paintings" in silk and delicate, fine brushstrokes. There were idealized images of women, women who looked like me, peacefully sitting down, holding their babies, or out in their gardens. One of my favorites was a painting called *"Jeune fille au chat blanc"* by Le Pho, which depicted a young woman holding a white kitty with one arm while pensively holding a cigarette in her other hand. There was a notebook on the table, and I imagined she had been writing poetry.

An idea came to me: I would research Vietnamese artists who lived in Paris. I settled on Nhat Toussaint, a mysterious Vietnamese painter who had moved to Paris in the 1940s. There hadn't been much written about him, so it would be, could be, my niche. I found him particularly compelling because he painted a lot of scenes of rice fields and mountains, which reminded me of Ninh Binh, the province where my grandparents lived and where my parents had grown up. Sitting in the white light of the library in Chapel Hill, what wouldn't I give up to return to that place right now? Feeling excited about my idea for the grant, I was even more pleasantly surprised when Oscar appeared before me. I had forgotten that we had agreed to meet up here.

"Hey there," Oscar said.

"Hey O. Can I call you that? O?"

"Umm sure."

"Do you have the French notes for me?"

"Uh huh."

He looked like he'd had a haircut recently. The grown-out curls had been replaced by a line-up.

"By the way, I like the haircut," I said, softening my tone.

He looked at me and shrugged awkwardly. Then, with a fake cough, he stuttered, "Well, here are your notes."

He looked like he was getting ready to go, so I quickly said, "Why don't you stay a while? Stay and do work here. I have to finish my grant proposal anyway."

Looking at me for a second, as if calculating the implications of our budding friendship and determining that he found it appealing, he pulled out a chair and sat down with gusto. We both laughed. Then he opened his laptop and we began to work. Although I had a scholarship for my tuition, not all projects were automatically funded. For a research trip fully funded by the Foundation itself, I had to type out a convincing research proposal. Otherwise, I assumed, the project could be interpreted as an excuse to wine and dine in Paris, which, in fact, was my ultimate objective.

Even though I hadn't found myself energized by schoolwork recently, applying for the grant revitalized me. I found myself typing up a storm, crafting a story about myself as a self-motivated young woman from Vietnam who dreamed of changing the world by unearthing the story of an obscure and unrecognized ex-pat Vietnamese painter. I highlighted the fact that I was proficient in French, having been in the French education system for 13 years before my move to the States. In the final paragraph, I wrote that I dreamed of one day opening my own art gallery which showcased Vietnamese art from different eras.

After an hour of sitting together in silence, except for the sound from our keyboards, Oscar closed his laptop. I finished the last sentence of my proposal draft and closed mine too. I smiled at him. He smiled back. "How'd it go? he asked.

"Pretty good."

He then asked me what I was hoping to do in the summer. I told him my project idea was to research a Vietnamese painter. When I started to tell him about the artist and his work, his eyes kind of glazed over.

"Oh. Cool," he said. He told me he lacked an artistic gene.

"That's impossible," I said. "Everybody who has a beating heart has an artistic gene. Come with me to the next exhibition at the school's gallery. I have a feeling you'll like it."

"Okay. Sounds good," he said. "By the way, why did you skip French today?"

"Do you want to know the truth?" I asked him.

"Yes. I guess."

"The truth is, I fell asleep. I get like this sometimes. I'll fall asleep for 11 hours straight and it's totally beyond my control." "Woah." He looked at me in disbelief.

"Yep," I said. "I think I need to see someone about it."

"Were you always like this?" he asked.

"Not in high school. I guess I was too busy studying and prepping for college back then. But ever since I got to college...I sometimes feel like I'm not in control of my brain. And I feel tired all the time. It's like my body is catching up on all my emotions. But it's not so strange. In Vietnam, everyone naps after lunch. Everyone in the whole country. It's part of our culture."

"Not for eight hours though, I hope?" he said with concern.

"Yeah, no. I think I'm way past the normal realm. Even for a Vietnamese person."

I'd never talked to anybody about my chronic napping before and certainly never explained the culture of napping in Vietnam. It was the first time that I had acknowledged that ever since I'd gotten my "break" in college, my body felt like it was breaking down, like I was finally catching up on years of sleep.

"I would definitely go and see someone if I were you," he said. "Could be a virus," I replied.

Then he gave me the French notes. Apparently, I'd missed the class on Romain Gary's *La Vie Devant Soi*.

"Oh, dang it! That's one of my favorite books!"

Oscar said, "Mine too."

We were becoming best friends. But would it ever be more than that?

I took Oscar's suggestion to heart and found a therapist that was part of the Counseling Services at the school. I was like a drug addict. I loved my drugs. I didn't want to give up my drugs. Nevertheless, I knew that it was a problem.

"What you have is Complex PTSD," Sheena, my therapist, said.

"What's that?"

"It's what a lot of children go through when they have been through abuse, emotional or physical, in the past. Oversleeping is your bodily response to the surge of past emotions that have gone unprocessed."

"Oh."

"Have you ever heard of the fight or flight response?"

I shook my head.

"Well, there are actually four main responses to trauma: fight, flight, freeze, and fawn. The excessive sleeping you are going through is probably a freeze state, to stop you from re-enduring your perceived past threats."

"Alright. But I feel guilty because I never was physically abused. My mom never *hit* me."

"Studies have shown that parents who neglect their children or who abuse them emotionally actually may create more harm in their children than those who physically abuse them."

"Wow."

"Yeah. Physical abuse doesn't always entail the emotional manipulation that occurs with emotional abuse. No wonder you feel helpless right now."

"I feel so helpless. But why is it happening now? I was fine a year ago." "Now that you're an adult, I think you're finally coming to terms with what really happened. You couldn't fully when you were a child. And you probably forgave a lot of the things that were traumatizing to you."

"Hmm."

"So, what I'm going to suggest is that you come for therapy and EMDR alternatively on a weekly basis, and then we can assess whether the panic attacks and uncontrolled sleep don't change."

I thanked her and saying goodbye, feeling somewhat relieved that there was some truth behind my napping lifestyle.

***

Chapel Hill, a couple of months later.

"Oh my god! I got approved for Paris!" I squealed, feeling the excitement spread over my cheeks in a blush.

"That's so great," Sooji said. We were both in our beds. It was eleven pm on a Tuesday night.

"Have you heard back from your internship?" I asked her.

"Yep, I'm interning for a law clerk this summer."

"That's insane!"

"Don't be too impressed, LOL. My dad had a connection. It's one of his buddies' firm."

"That's still cool though." I couldn't judge Sooji, especially knowing that if I were in Hanoi, my mother would be doing the same. I had stopped pretending long ago that the rules of privilege and access didn't prevail. It was part of the deck of cards that I'd been dealt as a girl in upper middle class Vietnam. Now, I was a little jealous of Sooji and her access to jobs that I'd have to carve out for myself as a Vietnamese person abroad.

"And Oscar? What's he doing these days?" Sooji asked.

"Just working his butt off in compsci. I think he's landed a summer position at an investment bank."

"Damn, Oscar!"

"Yeah, I know, right?"

It seemed to me like everyone I knew was going into banking or consulting or law. Of course, I was doing what I loved, looking at art, and studying art. And yet, a part of me liked the idea of making a good income and then relaxing at a five-star resort. I wouldn't mind sending endless monotonous emails for hours at a time, or whatever a corporate job entailed, if it meant stability and independence. For all my talk of gratitude, I also resented my dependence on my mother for financial security.

It was funny how much my days had started to revolve around Oscar. He was three years older than me, and yet, when we were together, our conversations flowed seamlessly. One of our favorite things to do together was to attend galleries, museums, and art shows. Since the first time I dragged him to one (a Georgia O'Keefe early paintings exhibit at The Ackland Art Museum, our college art gallery), we had gone to see Henry Taylor, Hiroshi Sugimoto, and Leonora Carrington. At first, Oscar told me he couldn't relate to art—it was flat and not dynamic. However, the more shows we went to, and the more we talked about the art, the more he developed a sharp eye for nuance and meaning in the works.

"I wonder if one day you guys will end up together," Sooji said, laughing. "That's impossible!" I said. "I'm too messed up and barely patched up for someone like him," I said.

"Thuy, that makes no sense. And trust me, you're not the only person who has an anxiety or sleep disorder in America. Something like one-third or something of the population has some sort of mental illness."

"You're right. But I think he's too strict and logical. And I'm too flowy and depressed."

Sooji laughed. "Well, you know what they say: opposites attract." I wondered if there was some truth to what Sooji was saying. Maybe there was a possibility. Still, it would not come from me. I wanted to explore dating and men. I was still a virgin. It was on my to-do list as something I wanted to experience. But, I didn't want to burden my best (male) friend with the problem of my virginity! On the other hand, what are friends for?

Chapter Four

Chapel Hill, Spring 2015

I was at a bar near downtown Chapel Hill. The place had silver curtains and red lamps throughout. The shadows from the lights created dragon shapes on the curtains. It felt like Dracula's den. Like most of my classmates, I had a fake ID. Sooji had hooked me up with a person who made the fake IDs, and since then, I had been to bars to drink beer with Sooji and her friends. But this was my first time at a swanky cocktail bar.

The dude who I was meeting here was the second guy that I matched with on Tinder, a Chinese guy named Nick. According to his profile, he was a 28 year old lawyer. He was five foot five, but since I was barely five foot two, I didn't mind shorter guys. Even though it was our first date, I had hopes of meeting my fairytale Prince Charming. I wanted to be swept off my feet, brought to a castle, and ravished. Did it sound stupid? Yes, I tried to tell myself. It was a first date and only that. The waiter put a glass of water in front of me. "I'm waiting for someone," I told him, suddenly nervous. Who was I to go on a date with a lawyer? I had nothing to my name. I was a freshman with mild-grade depression and a tendency to fall asleep for way too long.

"Hey. Thuy, right?"

I almost choked on my water. "Yes. Yes I am. Nice to meet you." He was a plain looking guy, not at all the slick dude in his profile picture. It looked like his receding hair had recently been trimmed at Supercuts. I looked into his eyes, as my mother had taught me to do when meeting people for the first time. He had a cold gaze, like he was at a business meeting or work. I tried to let my initial aversion go. After all, what experience did I have with men? We talked about the usual - the weather, what he did for work, where we were from. He told me his life story: his parents were doctors on the West Coast, their disappointment when he decided to study law. "It was shocking to them, if you can believe it." It was my turn, and I told a condensed version of my life: "I grew up in Hanoi, when I was fifteen I moved to Pennsylvania for boarding school, and now I'm at UNC on a scholarship."

"Neat," he said. He looked kind of bored. I felt annoyed that he didn't seem more impressed by my temerity and academic accomplishments, but tried to not show it. He glanced at his phone, and I could tell he was checking the time. What little hope I'd had for the evening was quickly dissipating. He ordered a glass of Cabernet Sauvignon and I did the same. When the drinks came, I took a large gulp. "Yum," I said, and then immediately felt embarrassed. He talked some more about his work; his voice had a stultifying monotony, and I started zoning out. When he asked me what I was studying I said, "Oh I don't know yet. Maybe Monet or Manet," just to shut him up. Plus, I remembered my mom telling me that men didn't like smart girls. He went back to talking about himself. His practice was focused on property law and he worked for an insurance company. "You won't

believe the things that people will try to claim in their insurance," he said. "People will set their house on fire and then try to make it look like an accident. I see it all the time." I was incredulous. I mean, I didn't think that there were that many people torching their own house for insurance money.

"Oh, I'm probably boring you," he said.

"Oh no," I replied. By then, I had finished my glass of wine and felt quite pleased with myself. I felt flushed and could tell from my underarms, which were hot, that I had started to get red. At least, since he was Asian as well, he probably wouldn't judge me for having the Asian flush.

"Thank you for a wonderful first date," I said as I abruptly got up, intending to leave.

At that instant, he reached out and grabbed my hand. "Oh, don't go," he said. I felt a certain weakness for the man. If at first, his gaze had seemed cold and corporate, now it was desperate. What the hell, just go with it, I coached myself. I texted Sooji to ask if I could have the room to myself.

"WTF!!" she texted.

"Yes," I replied.

"Ok!! Only if ur sure. Be safe!!!" she texted, and then I invited Nick back to my dorm room D.

We had sex on my thin mattress. At first, I was nervous, and my mind repeated the thought: *I'm a virgin, I'm a virgin.* He had a short torso, which made his face seem disproportionately big. When he put it in, it only hurt for half a second before I stopped feeling anything. I went to the dark abyss in the center of my chest where I hid all of my painful emotions. "I'm gonna cum!" he half shouted. Afterwards, he took off the condom and got up to throw it in the trash can, while I lay in bed, thinking about how underwhelming the whole thing was. He came back and tried to kiss me, but I pulled my head away. He sat there quietly for a few minutes. "Nice meeting you," he said awkwardly. Then he got dressed and left.

Later, Sooji asked me how it went.

"Meh," I said.

"You're so nonchalant about it, I'm surprised," she said.

"I guess. But I felt bad for him, so I just did it."

She shook her head.

"Thuy, you don't have to let any man into your body if you don't want to." "For some reason, it didn't seem like that big a deal to me at the time," I said. "And he had a desperate look."

"You can't just do things because people want you to," Sooji pleaded. "Please tell me you won't have sex again just because you feel bad," she said. "Just call me and I'll pull you out of it, okay?"

"Okay," I said.

Even though the sex was consensual, I immediately regretted getting physical with a guy whom I barely knew. I was *a bad, bad girl,* the internal voice inside of me kept saying, the same voice that had carried me through my childhood years.

***

Hanoi, 2003

The first thing I heard was Mom throwing the phone on the floor.

"What did you say to me?" she shouted at my father in our living room.

I couldn't understand exactly what they were fighting about. Mom was throwing around numbers about a deal that wasn't going like she'd expected. "This is YOUR fault!" she screamed. "You're a useless piece of shit!"

My dad, as usual, stood on the sideline completely mum.

Mumbling, he said, "Look, it was a bad deal from the get-go—anybody could have seen it from a mile away."

"Shut the fuck up!" she replied.

I looked at the phone on the ground, and my heart thudded at the sound of her voice, high pierced and shrill. When I returned to my bedroom, I felt the same pain that I'd felt yesterday and the day before that. There was no peace in this house. That night at dinner, we were all quiet. It was the norm in our household to let Mom have her burst of anger while everyone else sat on the edge of their seats. No one spoke. I ate fried spinach with garlic and fried rice. Even though the tumult had died down since this morning, I anticipated more conflict. After dinner, I brought the plates and bowls to the kitchen for our maid, Tina, to take care of. I found Mom in her bedroom and gave her a hug. I wanted to feel closer to her - to make her feel better about whatever struggles she was having with my dad. She pushed me away. "Stop, I'm on the phone," she said. I found Dad in the living room watching TV. I sat down on the couch next to him. I wanted to cry. I wanted to scream. He reached out and took my hand and gave it a squeeze. I looked over at him and noticed the tears running down his cheeks.

The Napper

***

I felt disgusted after the hook-up I'd endured the night before. It was yet another doofus, this time an IT specialist who worked in the library. The same cycle repeated itself—I didn't intend to have sex, but once I was in his dorm room, I felt bad, so I slept with him. It wasn't like I was there physically. Instead, I could see it all from above. I could literally watch myself having sex. *It doesn't mean anything.*

In French class, I felt like there were huge rocks stuck inside my rib cage, and that they were on fire. The constriction I felt in my chest at the place where all my heavy and uncomfortable emotions had been locked away all these years was more acute than ever. I could hear what the teacher was saying - something about the Maupassant story we'd been assigned to read. My head started to ache. *It's not that bad,* I told myself. *Just stop complaining and focus.* I made an effort to relax with everything that I had, but my body felt tighter and tighter, and the pain in my chest throbbed. Using a technique that I'd developed as a child, I imagined that the pain and discomfort were just part of a dream. *I'm okay,* I told myself, shutting down as much of the emotion as I could. The result was a sensation of numbness. By the end of class, I couldn't wait to go back to the dorm and sleep. If there was nothing that could help, and nobody that understood me, sleep was always there, my faithful friend.

"Hey, are you alright? You seem off," Oscar said as we were walking out of class.

"Yeah, I'm alright," I replied, picking up my pace. And then, just as I was walking ahead of him, my legs and vision gave out on me.

"THUY!" I could hear from far away.

When I woke up, I was lying on a bed in the health center. I saw Sooji and Oscar sitting there, worried looks on their faces. Oscar was holding my right hand.

"Hey sweetie, how are you feeling?" Sooji asked.

"What happened?" I asked.

"You passed out right after class," Oscar said. He seemed distraught.

"It felt like I was having a panic attack," I said. "That's all I can remember." "The doctor says you had really low blood pressure," Sooji said. "Have you been eating at all?"

"I have," I said.

"You need to take better care of yourself," Oscar said.

At some point, I must have fallen asleep again, and when I woke up, the clock said that it was 5:00 p.m.

A nurse came in to get my vitals.

"You passed out from dehydration and low blood pressure dear," she said, handing me some Gatorade to drink. "Your friends told me that you said it felt to you like a panic attack?" I nodded.

"Do you have a therapist?"

I nodded again.

"Okay, well, I'd recommend that you schedule a meeting with your therapist soon, and perhaps even a psychiatrist."

"I will," I said.

"You're free to go after you eat that pudding. I'll also give you a student meal to take home and finish."

"Thank you."

As I prepared to leave, she commented that I was lucky to have so many friends in my corner. "Your guy friend especially was very worried. He kept badgering us nurses about your vitals. I had to tell him it was confidential. I could only tell him that you were fine and taking a nap."

I laughed.

"He gets like that sometimes."

I walked back to the dorm, my stomach grumbling. In our room, Sooji got up from her desk where she was doing some homework. "Here she is, you got us all so worried!" she said, her voice relieved, giving me a big hug. I sat down at my desk, munching on the food in the plastic container that the nurse had given me, meatloaf with tomato sauce and broccoli. It tasted like

dirt, but at least it was salted.

"Ew," I said.

"You better eat up lady, doctor's orders," Sooji said like a good mother. "Thanks," I replied. I was grateful to have a friend like her. I wasn't used to having many friendships. Girlfriends or friends who were female tended to be difficult for me. For the first time, I felt like I had someone in the States who felt like family.

Chapter Five

Chapel Hill, May 2015

Oscar and I had a class presentation together. We were supposed to present a French song and potentially sing it. It was such a lame assignment.

"Doesn't this sound childish to you? What are we? In beginning level French?"

"I dunno, I guess Louisa is trying to end the year on a lighter note," he said.

"It is a bit stupid, you gotta admit."

"Not to me! I'm totally drowning in my compsci final assignment. I can totally use something easy."

Usually, we'd be studying in the library, but because of the musical nature of the assignment, we decided to meet at Oscar's apartment instead. He lived in one of the better-looking luxury apartments on the east side of town. His place was clean and neat, just as I'd expected, and the kitchen was newly upgraded with fancy black appliances and a marble countertop. There was a new velvet olive green sofa in the living room, and he had his own bedroom and bathroom.

"How do you afford this place?" I asked. I was wondering about the cost of renting an apartment, as I wanted to move into an apartment with Sooji next year.

"I have side gigs," he said. "I'm working remotely for a green juice start-up doing computer coding."

"Ever the industrious man," I said, then, after a pause, "Let's get going on this stupid song." I had a date later that night. A guy named Dan who played on the lacrosse team at Duke, or so he said. He was good-looking, in an Aryan kind of way. I wasn't quite sure if I had a type, but since I'd lost my virginity, I'd been sampling. It was like a research assignment. I hoped the hook-up sex would make me feel something. Help me come out of my slumbering state of mind. But to no effect.

We pulled up the list from Google of the *59 Best French Songs of All Time*. It was a bunch of love songs, but then I found one that called out to me. "Let's do Francoise Hardy's *Tous Les Garçons et Les Filles*!" with as much enthusiasm as I could muster. Oscar pulled his guitar out and he sounded like an angel. We practiced singing the song for the next hour. I really related to the last verse of the song. With emotion, I sang in French: "The day that I will no longer be a lost soul that day that I, too, will get someone who loves me."

When we finished singing, Oscar turned to me and said, "Thuy, I think I'm in love with you."

"What?!" I said. I was speechless. I don't know why, but I was not expecting this. I had been used to closing off my heart. I didn't think anybody else could open theirs to mine.

"I love you, Thuy," he repeated, now in a more serious tone.

"Oscar, you can't just say things like that!"

"Why not?"

"Because! I don't know how to react!"

I felt my face flush. For some reason, meeting strange men on the Internet was easier for me than sharing my feelings with a friend whom I cared for.

"You don't have to know how to react," he said.

Standing in front of him, I looked into his deep brown eyes. And a flutter of happiness rose in me.

"Can I kiss you?" he asked.

I nodded my consent, then felt his soft lips on mine. We moved closer to one another, and I felt his warm hands on my back. It was funny. You hang out with someone for days on end and you become their friend. Then, once the friendship veers into romance, it's as though your whole body had been familiar with their body all along. We moved onto his bed. Again, more kisses. I felt entwined with him, his smell, our bodies facing each other side by side.

"Were you surprised by what I said?" he asked me.

"I mean, I guess so…" I said.

"Why?"

"I never saw myself as more than a friend to you."

"I literally hang out with you every day. We study together and we eat together."

"Sooji is always going around nagging me about how we should be together.

I thought she was crazy."

"So do you think we're together then?"

I gave him a look and raised my eyebrows.

"I have no clue what you mean," I said.

"Will you be my girlfriend?"

Once again, I nodded yes.

When I got back to my room later, I told Sooji about everything that had happened.

"I guess he doesn't know about all your Tinder hookups!"

"Sooji!" I squealed.

"Just kidding. Now you'll have a man who treats you right. Plus, he's going into investment banking so-great pick! He'll make a great husband, even if he'll be working like a bull for the next five years."

"Trust me, I am not thinking that far ahead."

The Napper

Sooji went to her volleyball practice, and I opened up my laptop to do more work. Having an athletic friend had made me realize how sedentary a life I was living, and that I ought to do more. Move my body some. My therapist had also recommended I move my body more. And I knew she certainly was not suggesting I move my body by hooking up.

Twisting and turning in bed as I tried to fall asleep, I wondered what types of girls Oscar had dated in the past. Perhaps he was too serious to date frivolously like I did. I was either trying to escape life (napping) or trying to gulp it all down in one bite (sex with random men). Both behaviors seemed aligned with broken parts of me. Oscar, however, was positive and optimistic. We were an odd match, that was for sure. I wondered if I would find a way to sabotage our relationship.

***

Now that I was officially Oscar's girlfriend, he wanted to do everything together. It was unfamiliar to me, having never had a boyfriend before, and being somewhat of a recluse.

"You know I'm like a sloth right?" I said when he woke me up at 8 a.m. in his bed.

"Come on, it's Sunday, let's do something fun." He took me to the botanical gardens near Duke University. Then we got brunch at the Nasher Museum of Art at Duke.

"You look forlorn," he said.

"I just feel like I'm trying to get myself together but it's not working out," I told him, pushing my eggs Benedict around. The meds that I had started taking for my anxiety worked some, but they left me more lethargic than ever. Nap lifestyle was in full effect.

"What do you mean?"

"Just, you know, I never thought life would catch up to me, but it did." I'd told him about my depression, and how I had tried to run from it by excelling in school. But it had only worked for so long before I crashed and burned right at the start of my college career, when I arguably needed to focus the most.

"Well, I think you just need some lovin' up on you," he said, and held my hand.

We finished the afternoon by renting a car and driving to a local dairy farm, one of the most beautiful parts of Chapel Hill. On the drive, the verdant green hills and springtime tulips lulled me and I had a delicious micro nap. When I awoke and saw the beautiful scenery, I was moved. A strange development, since not too long ago I'd been numb to everything.

In the evenings, we'd kiss, bodies entangled. I wanted to rush to intercourse, like it was a fast-food meal. But Oscar was slow and tender. He swooned over every part of my body. After the first time we had sex, I started sobbing. All the emotions came up for me all at once. He hugged me and let me get it all out. For the first time ever, I felt like the cement walls around my heart were slowly breaking down. I had thought that when my best friend turned into my lover, everything would be terrific. Except things aren't always so simple. And I wanted more. More fire, more excitement, more connection.

In March, I was notified that my research grant to Paris was approved.

Oscar was overjoyed. He was going to be working for an investment bank in New York over the summer, but was determined to pay me a visit while I was in Paris. We celebrated the end of the year by going out to dinner.

"Are you excited for the summer?" I asked Oscar over pad thai.

"Yes, definitely," he said in a rather serious tone. "I want to land a job by the end of the summer, and then start my career right after college."

Lately, he'd seemed stressed to me. I wanted to help him feel better, but all I could do was tell him that it was going to be alright.

"Hey Oscar," I said, finally bringing up what was weighing on my heart, "Maybe it's better if we took a break this summer."

"A break?" he said, shocked.

"Yes, I don't think I can focus on my research with us. It's all been lovely so far, but I feel like I need to be selfish and focus on myself."

I expected him to be upset, maybe to cry, to fight back. Instead, as if he knew there was no point in pushing me, he only said "You're fucking cruel," and got up and left the restaurant.

I wanted to run after him, but I didn't. As always, I expected life to work itself out somehow.

That night, Sooji wanted me to explain.

"What the hell?!?" she said, once she heard about our break-up.

"I don't know what happened…I mean, I do, but…" I said, unsure of how to phrase it without sounding like a coldhearted bitch.

"Thuy - this guy treats you like a queen, you spend all your time together, he clearly LOVES you. And I thought you loved him too? Or are those googly eyes of yours a lie?"

I gave her a stern look that said "Really?"

"That's a bit harsh, isn't it?" I said.

"Well then, explain it to me!"

I lay down on the bed. Stared up at the ceiling of our dorm, the big ugly whiteness of it, and thought about all those hours waiting for life to happen, first in Hanoi, and then in boarding school. When was life supposed to begin? I'd always felt so insecure when I was young that I'd never dated anyone. I remember the one nerdy Orthodox Jewish guy at The Hill who'd asked me out. On our date, he'd confessed that the kind of women he was interested in were blonde shiksas. "But you'll do, " he said, laughing. The days I spent with Oscar felt so peaceful and calm. But he was the kind of man that I found myself wanting to befriend. He was reliable, and dependable, someone I could lean on to provide camaraderie and easy laughs. But as a girlfriend, I had felt awkward around him. Friendship had provided a layer of protection from hurt, from harm, or so I imagined. Plus, I did not feel worthy of having another person care for me without asking for anything in return. I was more comfortable with friends who wanted me to help them with their essays or who needed some other kind of help.

Oscar had taught me that you could be loved for who you were. And you could say that I loved Oscar. I was very much attracted to him. How could I not be? I was impressed that he had a goal and a plan for life: to work in investment banking, to help his mom, to help pay for his sister's tuition. Maybe I was especially impressed since I was somewhat directionless. And then, when we got together romantically, I kept waiting for the other shoe to drop. I got so anxious at times, that I thought perhaps it would be better if we stayed friends rather than continued as lovers.

Of course, I could not explain any of this to Sooji. I didn't think she'd understand my need for alone space even as I desperately craved love and affection.

I simply said, "I don't know Sooj, it just didn't work out."

"I hated all those other guys you brought home," she said bluntly, sounding like she was hurt on behalf of Oscar.

In bed that night, I replayed the scene of the breakup over and over in my head. The bad girl, the girl who always ruined things. The girl who hurt people. Once again, I had proven to myself—and the world – that there was something inherently bad in me. In a way, I had saved Oscar from the bumbling, depressing mess that I was. The next day, I ate some ramen and napped. I just had to make it until Paris.

Chapter Six

Paris, End of May 2015

I got the grant check for Paris (eight thousand dollars, thank you, scholarship donors!), and decided that besides writing an article about Nhat Toussaint, I would do four things:

Eat baguettes and cheese Meet up with my childhood best friend June.

Get myself into some sort of EPIC Parisian romance—nothing less than a mind-blowing emotional and sexual connection.

Stop thinking about Oscar. No, we hadn't talked since the break-up, and I know I needed to be the one to reach out first, but something always stopped me.

All those years of being platonic with boys in boarding school had created something of a monster. Now, I only wished to indulge in pleasure in all of its forms, sexual or not. Who was to blame? I was a young girl from Vietnam who'd moved to the U.S. to chase the American Dream. I worked like a beast. I took every single A.P. class I could. The humanities classes fit my natural aptitude, but I also took AP Physics and AP Calculus, even though I barely understood the material. Until my depression caught up with me. I remember my AP Calc BC teacher asked me if I had just "made up" answers on my exam. I tried my best not to flat out answer *yes*. God bless the Korean and Chinese kids in the class who volunteered to tutor me, because otherwise, I would not have made it. I'd also stay up all night doing the practice exams for SATs. Once the security guard of the dorm went to check the common hall of the dorm and saw me still typing at 3:00 in the morning. Outwardly and academically, I was successful, but inwardly, I felt inept, that I lacked in all departments. That summer, I made a pact with myself: it was going to be the summer of self-reclamation.

My first morning in Paris, I went to the first bookstore I could find. It was a short walk from my friend June's apartment in the 20th arrondissement. I took it as a sign from the universe when in the storefront window, I saw *The Passions of Jean Baptiste*. I thought to myself, *I need to find a man that looks like the tortured, grimacing man on that book's cover.* I needed to find someone as messed-up as me. Possibly more. There are no expectations with two messed-up people.

Unlike an American bookstore clerk, the clerk of this shop, an old man with tiny gold-rimmed glasses, did not say hello or acknowledge my existence. There was no music playing, and whatever conversations that took place were held in a whisper. I was in my element. I valued silence, a trait that seemed non-existent on the other side of the Pacific. And I had a strange connection to the French because of my earlier education. And because they had once occupied my country. But like every other power that tried it, they got their asses handed to them. In the bulky art books section, I flipped through a Sophie Calle book and a photobook of the last years of René Magritte. I loved this quote in the René Magritte book: *"My painting is visible images which conceal nothing; they evoke mystery and indeed, when one sees one of my pictures, one asks oneself this simple question, 'What does that mean?' It does not mean anything, because mystery means nothing, it is unknowable."*

I ended up with Clarice Lispector's *Near to the Wild Heart*, and a print of Magritte's *The Lovers II*.

June wasn't home, but she had left her keys at the coffee shop next door.

She was in class at one of the most prestigious art schools in Paris, École des Art Décos. We were going to meet for a pho dinner, which I was looking forward to. It was commonly accepted that the Vietnamese community in France excelled culinarily, more than any other Vietnamese expat community.

I knew I would adore Belleville from the moment I arrived. I felt at ease knowing that I would get to speak French. Then there was seeing other Chinese and Vietnamese people just living their regular lives. And nothing made me happier than seeing a bunch of Asian grocery stores and restaurants. That was something that I'd never let go of - the way food gave meaning to life, something you learned without a doubt growing up in Vietnam.

"*O la la! Salut Thuy!*" June said.

Gorgeous as ever, she was tall with a short pixie haircut. I always envied her eyes, which were almond shaped and exaggerated with dark eye makeup, making her face look foxy and her looks stern. We exchanged a big hug and cheek kisses.

"*Regarde-toi là!*" I said to her. Even though we were Vietnamese, we always spoke in French when we were together, ever since childhood.

"Do you think I've changed?" I asked her. I felt more attractive since I had lost the weight I'd gained in high school.

She took a second to look me up and down.

"Yes," she pronounced. "You definitely look more grown up."

I told her that I thought that she looked the same. While she still bore a resemblance to the tall, gangly

Vietnamese girl I'd known, she'd become even more attractive, if that was possible.

We talked about our work and relationships. She was working on an upcoming painting exhibition.

"I'm excited to have you stay with me for the summer," she said.

"Yeah, thanks for hosting me," I said. I had always adored Belleville, where she lived.

"So, what's up with you these days?"

I told her everything, how I'd declared art history as my major, my plan to research Nhat Toussaint, and even Oscar.

"We broke up," I told her. It had been a short few months of intense connection followed by total destruction, and hook-up sex with strangers afterwards.

"Yikes!" she said.

"Yeah, no shit," I said, then we laughed.

"I mean, out of all my friends, you'd be the last person I'd imagine to be a slut!"

"Bitch!" I said.

We laughed so hard that I feared we'd annoy the other customers. But it was a Vietnamese restaurant, so they'd probably feel happy that two Asian girls were having a good time.

I told her my game plan.

"You're crazy," she said. "Frenchmen are not that great."

"You're literally dating one," I said.

"LOL, you're right."

After our delicious dinner (I'd gotten the *pho bo tai* and she'd gotten *bun bo hue*), I received a message from Oscar.

"Call soon?" he texted.

"Yeah," I replied.

We agreed to Facetime once I returned to the apartment. Why did I think it was a good idea to Facetime? But that's what I did. He was as gorgeous as ever, and those large doe-eyes, damn! I missed him. He no longer had the heart-broken face he'd worn the last time I'd seen him.

"You look well," I said.

"You too."

"How's Paris?"

"I just got here, but it's beautiful. As you know." Oscar used to spend summers in Paris visiting his extended family.

"Right," he was finishing up some work on his laptop as we spoke.

"I'm sorry," I said. "I never meant to hurt your feelings."

"No, it's fine," he replied. "Also, I started dating someone else." My heart dropped, but I did my best to put on a smile.

"Oh really? Tell me about the girl!" I said, faking excitement.

"Her name is Jennifer. She's a co-worker."

"Naturally," I said.

We talked for a good hour. He even seemed happy for me when I told him about my plan to explore my sexuality in Paris.

"Don't forget about your research," he said, sounding like a stern brother.

"Don't you worry," I replied.

He smiled, and I thought that my plan better pan out if I was giving up this perfect man for it.

"By the way," I asked him. "Are you still planning on coming to Paris?"

"Yeah, I mean, I booked non-refundable tickets."

"Oh, cool," I said. When we hung up, I felt like everything was just as it should be. Oscar was with someone else, someone much more dependable and stable and HAPPY than me. And I had a whole summer in Paris to myself. Maybe I wouldn't even need to nap as much. It was time to wake up from my slumber.

***

June and I were just hanging out at a bar, drinking gin and tonics and smoking. I could see a table of two men out of the corner of my eye, one white and one Asian. The white man had a short mustache and glasses. The Asian man was taller, and he was reading *L'Équipe*.

"I bet one of the guys is into art like you," June said. June had been trying to play matchmaker wherever we went. I felt embarrassed around her because she was more mature and freer around men than I was. When we'd been in school together in Hanoi, by the time we were in sixth or seventh grade, June had started dating boys. I remember watching her around boys in class; she had no problem with them. It also was when our friendship started to change and we separated. She found other friends who were also dating. I, in the meantime, was getting more and more serious about school, studying hard to get my grades up. I barely had time to look at boys because I spent all day with my head down in my books. For some reason, I had always been afraid that I'd have to drop out because school did not come easy for me.

I asked June for a smoke, but when she gave me a cigarette, she couldn't find her light.

"Do you ladies need help?" the man with glasses asked.

We looked at each other and smiled. He seemed like my type: nerdy and charming.

"Sure, thank you," I said.

He lit my cigarette and I took a puff.

"Would you like to join us?" June asked.

Glasses guy smiled and pulled a chair over. His name was Richard, and he owned an art gallery.

"No way!" June almost shouted. "My friend Thuy here is majoring in art history."

"Really?" he said.

"She's researching Nhat Toussaint."

"I have several of his pieces at my gallery," he said. "You'll have to come by and check them out." If I was a fan of this guy's looks, I was that much more impressed that he had Toussaint in his gallery.

Richard's gallery was in the first arrondissement, not too far from the Louvre. He only happened to be in Belleville because he was getting *banh mi* with his friend. I asked him what kind of *banh mi*. He said the classic one with Vietnamese ham, basil, and lots of chili pepper sauce. I smiled, approving his choice.

The next day, after waking up, I ate a bowl of granola, yogurt, and berries at the local café. I sat at an outside table and watched people stroll by. I loved Belleville because it almost reminded me of the laid-back environment of Hanoi. People here were dressed better than in the States, and they walked with a more relaxed gait.

After breakfast, Richard and I met at a café near his gallery, both of us downing an espresso. Then we walked past the Louvre and the Jardin des Tuileries, where one could hear the shouts of children, and their mothers calling to them. There were Parisians taking a smoke break next to groups of Chinese and Japanese tourists taking selfies. His gallery resembled more a studio more than an actual gallery. Near the entrance, paintings were lined up in a disorganized manner. Once you walked in, many pieces of art hung on the walls, almost all of Asian origin. A couple of Nhat Toussaint pieces that I'd been looking at in books were indeed on the wall. "My goodness," I said, impressed to see this work in person finally. There was a painting that I particularly admired: a woman sitting at a desk smoking and holding a black cat. It resembled the Le Pho's painting that I adored, but in this painting the woman face was brushed over, as if she was disappearing in front of my eyes. I thought it was an ingenious move as it gave off a sense of eeriness that I particularly enjoyed in art.

"This one's my favorite," I told him.

"Yes, an early Nhat Toussaint," he said. "The early paintings were traditional, more delicate – figures of beautiful women drinking tea and writing calligraphy. Unlike his later work which, well, as I'm sure you know…"

"Yes, I know." Nhat Toussaint's later paintings were mostly nudes, totally giving the finger to the traditional Confucian values of propriety and modesty. It indicated the artist's wish to carve out his new identity as an immigrant in France. He walked me through more of his collection, telling me about the sale of a big collection of Vietnamese paintings at Sotheby's in the 90s; he'd bought them all for a good price. It made me wonder if art was even his main interest.

"Does this mean that you do this for fun?" I asked him.

"Yes," he said. "I have to say it's one of my more hands-on projects."

"So, else what do you do?"

"I do financial investment consulting. I also own a vineyard in the South of France, a business in the Balkans, and I also do venture capital investing." "Right," I said, feeling out of my league.

We looked through the rest of his collection. He said that I could stay as long as I'd like to look at the four Nhat Toussaint paintings.

"Why Vietnamese art?" I asked him.

"My parents were diplomats, so we moved around a lot. I lived in Hanoi for five years," he said.

"No way, I'm from Hanoi," I said, pleasantly surprised. Even though I didn't want to return to the city due to my family, I loved my hometown. If it wasn't for the traumatic memories, I'd never have left in the first place.

"I know," he said.

"What gave it away?" I asked him.

"You remind me of my first girlfriend. She was also from Hanoi, and she talked like you. Confident but with a cool remove." Our eyes locked. I could see a hint of desire in his eyes. I was sure we would meet again. "I have to run to a business meeting. I trust that you can take care of yourself here?"

I nodded yes and we exchanged phone numbers. After he left, I pulled up a chair and sat in front of the Toussaint's, taking notes on the composition, the elements of erased or at times hidden faces in his subjects, and comparing them with the notes that I'd already taken. I had to thank the god of synchronicity. Each of the four paintings was essential my research question. They were from the four major phases of his life: a young student in Hanoi, his early years in Paris, his later travels, and his permanent relocation to Paris. As a teenager he'd studied in a French art school in Hanoi, and absorbed one simple orientalist view of Vietnamese art (art which depicted an idealized Vietnam, without the effects of colonialism). His travels across Europe and abroad, where he would study techniques from Paul Gauguin and Jean Fouquet, began his vision of modern Vietnamese Art.

By 4:00 p.m., feeling quite proud of myself, I began to clean up and position the paintings back where they'd been, thinking that if I wanted to rob the place, I'd probably make millions of dollars. I felt nervous, thinking that I should have worn gloves, but Richard had insisted that as long as I only touched the frames that I would not cause any damage.

"Dinner tonight?" Richard texted, and I said sure.

I had just enough time to go home to June and tell her the crazy story of what'd just happened.

"Now that's unfair!" June said.

"Ha, ha, it's probably nothing," I said. "I mean it's not like this is going to end up being anything substantial. I doubt he even lives here."

"But this is EXACTLY what you've been wanting, isn't it? A Paris affair. He's rich and sexy and he has the exact paintings you want to write about."

"I mean - yeah."

"Girl, you're onto something," she said. "By the way, how old is he?"

"Forty-two, I think."

"That's a twenty-three year gap."

"Yeah."

With that, we shared a glass of red, and then I took a nap before getting ready to meet Richard at 9:00 o'clock. We met at a swanky brasserie in the Marais. I was a little late, which is the Parisian way. It had a unique menu with Asian fusion touches, and the dimmed lights and many candles gave it a romantic ambiance.

"How did you like the collection?"

"Not like," I said. "Love, I loved it." Realizing that perhaps I sounded too eager and immature, I added, "It was quite impressive."

"I'm glad you liked it," he said.

I lit up a cigarette.

"Is there anything in particular you'd like me to order?" he asked.

I told him to go ahead and choose, that I ate anything and everything.

"But what do you like?" he asked.

"A filet mignon is never a bad idea."

"Don't mind me if I order half of the menu," he said.

"I won't mind at all." He ordered, and the waiter proceeded to bring out everything from steak tartare to tuna sashimi with truffle.

"What do you do in your free time?" I asked him over a mouthful of grilled, honey-dipped Brussel sprouts.

"I collect art," he said.

"Right."

"I also like cycling," he said. "That, perhaps, is one of the few things rarely related to work."

I built up the courage to ask him what had been on my mind.

"What are your wife and kids like?'

He smiled.

"My wife is well. She lives in Bordeaux with our two children."

It did not bother me in the least that he was married with children. If anything, it was a good thing. It meant I could always leave. And so could he.

And for good cause. The waiter came by and refilled our glasses of Bordeaux. Richard raised his glass.

"To your research summer in Paris," he said.

"Santé."

Later, he asked me if I wanted to come to his place for a night cap and I agreed. He lived in a two-story duplex in the St. Germain. A man at the front door greeted him as Mr. Britten.

Once inside, I was a bit awed. "This is an amazing house," I said. There were photographs on the wall of him on sailboats, playing soccer, riding horseback, and posing with famous artists. He presented me with a snifter of cognac. I took a big gulp and almost choked. Then we sat down on a white sheepskin loveseat in the living room, opposite a fireplace. We started kissing. Our kisses happened not in one long song but in little quips and bursts. Upstairs, in what was presumably the guest bedroom, there were floor to ceiling windows. There was a gorgeous view overlooking the trees that peppered the row of luxury houses. We sat on the bed. I put my head on his shoulder. He held my head in his hands and brought me closer to his lips.

"I'm not ready to have sex," I said. "But we can keep making out if you want."

"Sure," he said.

I felt feline, my skinny frame positioned over his. My thighs made a pyramid on top of him. Though I was small, I also felt strong, like I had control over him. Of course, I knew that he was much stronger and that if he wanted, he could hurt me. I felt his erection underneath his pants. For some reason, it felt more intimate to touch somebody through their clothes than naked. After a while, he held me.

"Richard?"

"Hmm?"

"Have you ever had an affair before?"

"Yes," he said. "Once, a long time ago - with a Spanish girl."

We kissed until we fell asleep. When I awoke, it was the next day. On the bedside table, was a note:

"Good morning, Thuy, I had to fly back to Bordeaux. Enjoy breakfast. The butler will take care of you."

In the dining room, was a spread of toast, butter, Greek yogurt, and strawberries. I wore the pyjamas that was left next to me on the bed. I didn't want to ask whose it was, but the Hello Kitty design on it made me guess it could have been his daughter's.

"Any coffee, mademoiselle?" the butler asked.

"Yes please."

"Cappuccino?"

"That would be wonderful."

I enjoyed my coffee before putting my dress back on and taking the train back to June's, where I took a long nap.

Chapter Seven

June asked me if I dated older men because I had daddy issues. I laughed and said, "No, I have mommy issues."

"How does that work?" she asked.

"I don't feel deserving of love, and I'm seeking my mother's love through men."

Sipping her drink, she said, "I guess that makes sense."

It had been a couple of weeks since my rendezvous with Richard, and we'd been texting in the intervening days. He gave me access to his gallery for my research, and it also became my writing space - much more private than the library or the dilapidated couch at June's. My research on Toussaint took a decidedly positive turn when Richard gave me Toussaint's daughter's email address, and we started writing back and forth. I was thrilled when she invited me to dinner at her place in the Latin Quarter.

June had been going often to École des Beaux-Arts to work on her paintings. In our apartment, sketch after sketch of male figures filled our space. Her art exhibition was happening on Saturday. Looking at her work, I asked,

"What are you trying to get at with these drawings of the male body?" "I think men's bodies are beautiful," she said. "I just feel like when men obsess over women's bodies, it's normal, but when we do it, it's somehow unseemly or a faux pas."

"Yeah," I agreed. I had seen my share of male bodies. The bodies of the men I had shared a bed with back in Chapel Hill, one after the other. I could barely remember their names. Of course, there was the body of the one person I did care for, Oscar. Even if there were not strong enough romantic feelings on my part, I was safe in his embrace - his beautiful, strong arms and steady heartbeat, which I would listen to in the early hours of the morning before going to class.

Emilie Toussaint lived in a charming little apartment next to the St. Chapel Church. I arrived at her house at 4:30 p.m., a little early. Still, it seemed better to arrive early than late. She looked like a librarian, with her red cat-eyed glasses, short curly hair, and vintage red-polka dot dresses. She had a refined, beautiful face with the same almond eyes as her father. Her bright red lips inspired in me a sense of admiration, a feeling that she had the maturity and confidence that I lacked.

"What's your article about?" Emilie asked me.

"I'm writing about your father's decision to leave Vietnam and settle in France. I want to know why so many talented painters decided to leave the comforts of their home to go to Europe."

"That's a great question," Emilie said. "Would you like some tea?"

"Sure, thank you."

Looking around the apartment, I didn't seem much art that I could trace back to her father, except for a few photographs of him on the walls. There was one in the hallway of a man with glasses that looked like him, holding a baby girl.

"Is that…?"

"Yes, my father is holding me. Most artists, male artists, are known to be horrible fathers and philanderers, but not my father. He stayed married to my mother for forty years until his death."

"Wow," I said, impressed.

We discussed her relationship with her father, and she told me stories about how he'd bring her to his studio as a child.

"I would sit in my corner, watching him paint. I loved every second of it."

I took notes about his relationship with Paris, his chosen city after Vietnam. "He said that he hated Paris before he came to love it. Although he talked about wanting to retire in Vietnam, he never did." With sadness in her eyes, she added, "He died of stomach cancer at the age of sixty."

She walked me into another room. It was almost as large as the living room and filled with sketches and paintings just sitting on the floor.

"I always wanted to do something with these. The people at Sotheby's have been calling me, asking about them. I wanted to sell them privately myself, but I don't have the time or the energy."

"Well, if you ever need an assistant," I said, "I'd be happy to help."

"Would you really?" she said with excitement.

She said that she'd love to have a Vietnamese person like me take care of the collection, especially someone with an interest in her father's work. As we were eating, she implored me to share more about myself. I told her my story. Hanoi, then Pennsylvania, then Chapel Hill.

"You're quite the traveler," she said.

"I guess you could say that."

"You remind me of my father," she said.

"That's very kind of you to say," I said. "However, I do not have as much visual dexterity as he."

"I don't mean art," she said. "I mean his gusto. You had the gusto to leave Vietnam. You followed your heart. That's why you left Hanoi for the U.S.,

Isn't it?"

"Yes," I said. I thought that somehow, this blonde lady with the small peacock brooch had insight into me.

"I always felt slightly ashamed that I had to leave home in order to find a place for myself," I said. "Sometimes, I feel like I betrayed my country for something which I'm not even sure about."

"Don't worry about that," she said. "If you're meant to end up somewhere, life has a way of bringing you to that place."

"You're right," I agreed.

We then started talking about our love lives. Emilie was not married. She had a companion who visited her twice a week, an architect, and they did not have children.

"What about you?" she said.

"I'm dating a married man, I'm afraid," I told her. My honesty surprised even me. I did not plan on sharing the story.

She laughed as if to say, *It is the Parisian way.*

"Oh, to be young," she said with a knowing eye. I didn't have to tell her that that married man in question was Richard. Of course, she would have known since they were friends.

"Well, I hope you enjoy yourselves," she said. "You deserve that." At the end of the night, she gave me some soup to take home and told me to email her so that I could help her organize her father's archive. I walked to the Montparnasse cemetery, wanting to look at the graves of Simone de Beauvoir and Jean-Paul Sartre. For a second, I felt pity at the thought of the great Simone sharing a grave. I had heard that she'd said her relationship with Sartre was her greatest achievement. Even if I were to love a man fully, I was the kind of woman who needed time and space for myself. At the very least, in death, I should hope.

Next, I made my way to the grave of Oscar Wilde and then the great.

Marguerite Duras. The way Duras wrote about shame, especially in *The Lover*, had always haunted me. Just like the protagonist who was swept away in illicit romances, I wanted to be taken away, ravaged, and swept up in a way that would destroy and then rebuild me. Shame. What a funny word. I felt shame, of course, sleeping with a married man, but was it wrong of me that the shame lasted only a few minutes after the act of making love? Or, in our case, making out. I wondered how my parents, who had survived the war and had worked their entire lives on my behalf, would feel, knowing that their daughter engaged in such activities. That their investment of money and time had resulted in these shenanigans. This was my rebellion. Perhaps rebellion and freedom were the same thing. And, if not this, then what had my ancestors fought for? Besides, I was the one who applied for and got the scholarships. I was the one who decided at the age of fourteen to leave my country. It was a fate that I had created for myself. Still, I could feel my

mother's moral condemnation all the way from Vietnam. Like Milan Kundera said, *"Your mother is your first communist dictator"* or something like

that.

It had been different with Oscar since we'd broken up. It was liberating to some degree because I had been, in my opinion, too dependent on him and his friendship. It was sad to admit this, but I did feel a bit better on my own. Maybe that was why I kept attracting men who didn't want to invest in me emotionally. It gave me the freedom I craved.

Oscar and I talked every other week. I was impressed hearing about all of the paid-for lunches and, of course, the pay itself. What would it be like, I wondered, to actually be paid for the work that you do? I'd need a job soon, but I also couldn't work in France or back in Chapel Hill because of my student visa. Growing up, I imagined myself to be lucky because I had parents who'd wire me money, but the older I got, the more I yearned to be financially independent.

"Are they hiring at the bank?" I joked.

"Thuy, you'd hate it here."

I laughed and asked about his mom and sister. They were both doing well.

Then I asked about his love life.

"Jennifer is great. Training for a marathon these days. So, I guess by default,

I'm also training for a marathon. And what about you?" he asked.

"I'm dating…a man."

"Oh, happy to hear." He raised an eyebrow, probably wondering how the hell another man would survive the kind of torture I'd put him through.

"Yes," I said. "His name is Richard."

"Richard," he said. "Solid name."

I left out the details about Richard's marriage and his children.

"You'll meet him when you arrive!" I said.

The Ritz in Paris was a collection of large, grandiose rooms in shades of cream, pale pink, and blue. From traveling with my family in Asia, I was not unfamiliar with luxury hotels, but I felt slightly unnerved by the rich brocades of the curtains and furniture. It reminded me of a class presentation I did on Louis XIV in fifth grade.

I was meeting Richard for dinner. He had texted me in the morning asking me what I was doing. I had just started working for Emilie, cataloging and filing the paintings. It had been almost three weeks since Richard and I had met, and I had been seeing other men, but none affected me to the degree that Richard did. I found him inside the beautiful Proust champagne bar. If there was anything that I liked, it was this: luscious, peach-colored sofas. "Hi, Thuy," he said as he stood up to pull a chair out for me. There was something overly convivial about him, and he seemed excited to see me. When the waiter came over, he asked for a bottle of Armand de Brignac Ace of Spades Champagne Brut Gold.

"So, what's new in your world these days?" he asked me.

"Well, I met Nhat Toussaint's daughter, and now she's hired me to be her

assistant."

"That's great! One of my buddies works at Sotheby's if you want to reach out to them as well."

"No way!" I said. It was a strange feeling that there was a place for me in this world.

"How are you?" I asked him. These few weeks of not seeing Richard and being away from Oscar had made me realize that there had been moments when I completely dropped the ball on the men in my life.

"I'm great. I just closed a couple of business deals."

"What kind?"

"Real estate in the South of France, and then the next batch of wines." Was it bad that I was impressed?

After all, I was the daughter of communists. But the materialist in me wanted to be swept away by a certain type of man who could provide these things. And even though she was a full-fledged member of the Communist Party, I knew I'd inherited these inclinations from my mother. My whole life up until this point, I'd felt like I was surrounded by people who had carved their own mythology, first my mom and now me. What was I trying to achieve?

"Tell me more about your plans," he said.

"I don't know," I told him. "I don't think I have any plans."

"You must," he replied.

"I'll tell you after I finish this glass of champagne!"

We laughed and drank champagne, and I had a couple of lavender and green tea macarons.

"What about you? What are your plans?" I asked him.

"I'm going to Dubai in a month. I'm an investor in a new hotel there."

"That's amazing."

I wondered whether I'd read any books about young women getting swept off their feet by rich men. Even if I hadn't, it wasn't difficult to imagine that these tales never ended well.

By that time, we had finished our bottle of champagne.

"Would you like to join me for dinner?"

"Sure, I'd love to."

Holding onto his arm, we walked into the main dining room. After stuffing myself with sea bream, fennel mousse, and rabbit with mustard, I was ready to go back to his place. But then, it suddenly started to rain, so he went to the hotel receptionist and got us a room. As soon as we entered the elevator, I jumped on him and wrapped my legs around his waist. I could smell his scent—a thick cloud of Oud.

In the hotel room, he asked if I'd like anything to drink, and I opted for water. He called room service, and when they delivered the mineral water, he poured me a glass.

I took off my ruffly pink dress, and he kissed me on the lips, making me feel a warmth between my legs. On the bed, he kissed my neck and caressed my breasts. It did not take long before he entered me, and I felt a wave of heat ignite within me. After we finished making love, we lay on the bed for a while.

"Do you know that you remind me of my Asian ex-fiancée?" he said. I felt a twinge of disgust but kept my mouth shut. Closing my eyes, I pretended that I was with someone who loved me, or at least parts of me. I needed to tell myself this to keep my emotions together. What else could I do? I was tired of digging holes and leaving myself in them. Yet, I felt a sense of safety in the darkness, a feeling that darkness was my best friend.

Darkness would keep me warm when Richard eventually left.

"Enjoy the room," he said not too long after we finished having sex.

I mumbled thank you and fell asleep.

The next morning, I woke up to a view of the interior courtyard. I wondered where Richard had gone, whether he'd gone back to his apartment and called his wife. Did she know that he'd been gallivanting this whole summer? I tried to shut down my paranoid thoughts about him having been with dozens of other women, young and attractive, probably prettier than me. I had initiated this rendezvous with the belief that I could be carefree and just use him for sex and the material experiences he could give me. But looking out my window, I felt a sense of despondency. Why was it that I kept attracting the wrong men? Or perhaps the right men in the wrong circumstances. In another lifetime, perhaps I would have met Richard in his late twenties, and we'd have fallen madly in love and had two and a half babies. I went into the bathroom and started a bath in the pale pink porcelain bathtub. A small window gave me a view of the hotel's indoor gardens. I sprinkled in lavender bath salts and lit the rose candle. When I sunk my body into the bath, my mind immediately returned to the events of the preceding night - how I'd enjoyed his mature body, strong arms, and the woody smell of his salt and pepper hair. It felt a bit wrong to have so much pleasure with someone who might just as well have been a stranger. That was what we were to each other - strangers who'd slept together, even if the intimacy of our physical exchange felt real. In every single touch, I imagined the loneliness and suffering of a man who was looking beyond the confines of his marriage for the touch of another woman. Perhaps he was a jerk and an asshole for hurting his family, but I put that thought cleanly out of my mind. The bath gel and shampoo were Maison Margiela's "Replica Jazz Club," and it smelled like the cologne that he'd had on last night. I wondered if I could just stay like this forever. Forever nineteen, skin forever soapy, bubbles sticking to my breasts and thighs.

The Napper

After the bath, I made my way to the phone on the nightstand and ordered a cappuccino. It cost 30 euros, a preposterous price. But I didn't have to pay, so what did I care? I watched the men and women in the courtyard from my balcony and sipped my foamy drink, feeling a tremendous sense of pleasure. Images of Richard's lips on my body, his tongue in my mouth, flashed through my mind. I had no clue when I'd see him next. This summer in Paris had been much more indulgent and sensual than I could ever imagine. The memories were, of course tinged with darkness, my friend and companion, a more reliable lover than any of these men.

Before I left, I went to the mirror and put on my Charlotte Tilbury "Pillow Talk" lipstick. There were dark circles under my eyes, and I looked like my mom after a long day of work. She'd get so annoyed at me as a child when I tried to cuddle with her, and she still had work to do. "Mommy, I look like you now," I said out loud as I looked at myself in the mirror, the same look of disgust that she'd given me so frequently now on my face.

On the train home, I had a headache and felt hungover. A long sleep awaited me at home. Before lying down, I stole one of June's cigarettes, no doubt she wouldn't mind and fell asleep to Elton John's "Amoreena."

Chapter Eight

I was working at Emilie's apartment, which, whilst charming and spacious enough in the way that mattered (with enough room for a hundred or so of Nhat Toussaint's paintings), was terribly disorganized. I tried to stay focused as I jotted down the important notes about each painting and categorized them by date, then by the periods of his career..

Around my fifth hour in the stuffy apartment, my stomach started growling. It was 2:00, and I decided to go out for lunch. On a leisurely stroll from the Latin Quarter towards Ile Saint Louis, I found a kitschy Irish pub and ordered a croque monsieur and an orange juice. Pulling out my notebook from my bag, I looked at my notes and imagined writing a small book on all of Nhat Toussaint's works. I wanted to write about his travels to and from his country of origin and around the globe, but mostly about his life in Paris. The project was becoming quite fruitful, with the potential of both establishing me in the art world in Paris and as a researcher.

After finishing my food, I walked back to the apartment. I wondered where Emilie had gone after handing me this job, wondering too if she even needed the money from the sale of her father's paintings. It had been almost fifteen years since his death, and she still had not finished compiling the catalog. I Googled Nhat and tried to look at previous sales of his paintings. There were a couple of his paintings that had sold at Sotheby's Paris for just over five thousand euros. Even without proper experience in the art auction world, I believed the paintings should have been valued at least ten, twenty times that. I took a screenshot of the paintings that had been sold and texted it to Richard, with whom I had not communicated

since our night at the Ritz.

"How much do you think these could sell for?"

"21.5 by 15.3 inches?"

"More or less."

"At least 280K US dollars."

"That's what I thought. I think Emilie was being ripped off, which is why she wanted to hire me and sell on her own. I feel like she should hire someone in the industry already, but she told me she was hurt by a financial advisor in the past, so she'd rather have me."

"I'm in Miami with my family. Perhaps next time I'm in Paris, we could meet up."

"Okay."

I ended the chat feeling both thrilled for Emilie and ashamed for my entanglement with the wrong man. I selfishly wished that Richard was here, that he could be more than a shadow of a fantasy, that he could become my fantasy itself –the rich businessman who swept me off my feet. Later, when I told June about my fantasy, she told me that I probably had that desire because my mother was a businessperson, and I never got her love.

"Classic, looking for our mothers in our partners," June said.

Frankly, I was sick of being psychoanalyzed by June.

Oscar flew into town on a rainy night in late July. He told me his flight would be slightly late. I had never picked up anyone from the airport before. I was only familiar with being picked up by our family's driver whenever I returned to Hanoi in the summer or for Christmas breaks.

Standing near the entrance to the terminal where Oscar was expected to arrive, I lit a cigarette, one out of the many packs I had bought in Paris. When June found out that I had started buying my own instead of stealing hers, she gave me a talking-to. "Don't you know you can get addicted?" she said while holding a burning cig between her fingers.

"I know, June, but it's only a European thing," I said, sounding blasé.

I wondered what Oscar would think if he saw me like this, smoking my third cigarette of the day. I had been anticipating his arrival, the way he always seemed to know what to say whenever I felt like the world was falling apart. An hour later, I found him at the luggage counter. He looked the same as ever, prim and proper, with his white button-up shirt and dark jeans.

"Hey, you!" I said, barely able to contain my excitement.

"Hey, Thuy," he said, hugging me. It gave me a sweet, overwhelming sense of familiarity and home, which almost brought tears to my eyes.

"I've missed you," I said.

"I missed you, too."

I tried to help him with his suitcase, but he wouldn't let me. We took a cab to June's apartment, where he'd be staying with us for the next two weeks.

"So, tell me, what's new with you?"

"Well, as I told you over FaceTime, I'm working hard with Emilie.

Toussaint and we've already started the first sales of her father's mid-career work!" I also told him that he needed to come with me to Emilie's home sometime and check out the art. He agreed. We talked a bit more about his summer in investment banking. He said that he found the job numbing yet tolerable because he was getting paid. He couldn't wait to reap the benefits of the major he'd chosen mainly for financial reasons. He said he wanted to start his own company, but he didn't know what yet.

"Maybe one day we could start an art auction house," I replied.

He said maybe and laughed. When we got to the apartment, I led him up the creaky flight of stairs.

"This is nice," he said, looking at our minuscule living and dining area.

There were some unwashed dishes on the coffee table.

"Apologies for the mess," I said.

"Nothing I haven't seen before." It was true; it was in my nature to be messy since my mind was always too focused on lofty ideals to care about cleanliness. The state of my home, no matter where I was, tended to reflect the scattered nature of my brain. While he got settled, I made a French press coffee and poured some into a small ceramic cup painted with little blue hearts. He took slow sips while I told him about my days in Paris, how I spent my time bouncing between the studio and drinks with June, and how the summer had ignited in me a heightened passion for my research.

"Any dating prospects?" he asked me. The way he paused before asking me made me think this was the question he'd been wanting to ask all along. "Well, there's somebody, but it's not like he's here full-time, so maybe it's nothing after all."

"What do you mean?"

"Well, for starters, he's married and doesn't live in Paris."

"Thuy!" Oscar said, practically shouting. He gave a long sigh. "This sounds like a bad idea."

"Well, one good thing about him is that he owns a gallery and has a couple of Nhat Toussaint paintings that were super helpful for my research."

"He seems fishy to me, Thuy," he said, shaking his head. Then, looking at my forlorn face, he added: "But who am I to judge? Maybe this is simply, as they say in French, *un rendezvous amoureux.*"

I laughed and agreed, "Yes, maybe that's what it is,"

I asked him if he wanted to go with me to the studio, but he said he needed to take a nap.

"We have some leftover beef bulgogi in the fridge if you're feeling hungry." He thanked me and then plopped himself on our purple couch. Before I left, I told him June was going to cook some food for us tonight as a celebration.

Seeing Oscar had made me feel a surge of loneliness, the kind that I hadn't felt in a while. Since my tryst with Richard, I had tried to go on a couple of dates, but each time would end early. The men were either too young or bored me with their small talk. I felt no tinge of romantic intrigue with them and didn't want to sleep with anyone with whom I didn't feel the intense connection I did with Richard. Perhaps I had developed a type, for better or worse. Old, rich, and unreliable. Funny enough, I harbored the delusion that Richard might change for me and we could have a future together. I didn't dare tell anybody that, not even June. But now that a former lover was in town–

someone who I had once loved–I felt the pain of my delusion. The man that I liked (loved?) was nowhere to be found.

I did not go to Emilie's studio as I'd told Oscar I would, but instead decided to text Emilie that I was sick and go to a bar near Richard's gallery. I wondered if there was a chance that he was in town, that we'd run into each other, and that he would confess to me his undying love. I imagined him telling me that he was leaving his wife for me. Immediately, my mother's voice said, "You silly girl, don't you know that men will only use you when it's convenient for them?" Tears came to my eyes. I was a silly girl playing a game I had no chance of winning. I acted one way—the happy, cool girl who wanted casual sex—but deep down, I desperately desired true intimacy.

I went into the tabac to get more smokes. The Arab guy at the counter nodded at me as he handed me a pack of Camel Turkish Golds. Sitting outside on the steps in front of a building, I got out my phone and re-read messages from Richard. It was as clear as day that he was only reaching out when it suited him. Was that what I was–a girl good for a meal and sex when the guy was in town? I suddenly felt disgusted with myself. It was what I'd wanted, wasn't it? The truth was I didn't know what I wanted. Sometimes, darkness came like a cloud, and she told me what to do. Self-destruction was the goal.

Yet, it would be dishonest of me to deny that Richard's lifestyle had a pull on me. I wanted to be the kind of woman who got wined and dined in exclusive hotels and restaurants. I wanted to be the kind of woman who lived in a private townhouse in St. Germain, who had a husband who owned multiple companies and gave her a large allowance. Growing up, I'd known of money and the pleasures that came from it. It was the only thing that my mother could give me. Emotional stability and safety – those were things that I didn't seek out. They were unfamiliar, scary, even dangerous.

I watched a young couple holding hands, walking ahead of me. They were teenagers who looked Chinese. The girl was leaning on the boy as she walked, almost like she wanted to be conjoined with him. When I was their age, all I could think about were my homework assignments and getting into a good school. When did it change? Why did it feel so gratifying to be held by Richard's gaze or feel his touch? Life was so confusing in so many ways. It felt like with every step I took forward in my professional life; I took ten steps back in my personal life.

That evening, I met up with Oscar at the brasserie near my apartment. Brasseries: something that I couldn't complain about. And nobody minded if I wanted to linger, which I did often, before and after work. Life felt slower here.

"That was nice of you to still come," I asked him. I was referring to our brief relationship and its quick break-up.

"I still wanted to see you, my friend," he said. "Plus the non-refundable tickets. Also, my cousins are in the Banlieue."

"I'm doing fine," I said, sipping a tiny cappuccino. "You know how much I wanted to get out of North Carolina."

"I know. And from your Instagram posts of your fancy nights out and all the wine, I would have thought you were an influencer."

I felt a bit awkward. While he was working hard to help his family, I had no worries except the men breaking my heart. That was a luxury that only rich kids had - to fuck around in Paris.

"You're living your Parisian dream life, aren't you?" Oscar asked. He crossed and then uncrossed his arms, looking uncomfortable. I wondered if he hated me for being spoiled.

"How's it going with you?" I asked.

"I'm good, you know," he said, but he sounded a bit unsure.

"But..?" I said.

While he darted his eyes, looking for an answer, I asked if he minded if I smoked. He did not.

"I guess I'm at the start of my career, and I should be loving it, but I don't."

"Hmm."

"Is it bad that I'm just doing it for the money?" he asked. Then, he immediately added, "I know it's good because I can provide for my future family and my current family, but I wish I could just disappear and do my own thing."

"Like what?" I asked him. I looked at his thick, bushy eyebrows, which had made me so attracted to him not so long ago.

"Like pottery. Like traveling."

"You are traveling," I reminded him.

"I guess so. I miss our evenings discussing French art and literature together."

"I thought finance interested you?"

He looked at me for a second. "It does. I just wish I had more free time."

For some reason, I felt the urge to reach out and hold his hand.

"I think you're great. You're a wonderful human being all around." And just like that, he reached over and kissed me. It was neither a peck nor a "make-out" kind of kiss, but something soft and passionate at the same time.

"I think I came all the way to Paris just to see you."

I blushed and started laughing—an inappropriate tic when I felt shy or embarrassed. But people often took it to mean that I was making fun of them.

"What's so funny?" he asked.

"You're funny," I said cryptically.

It was nice to again be with someone who wanted to be with me for me. We walked the long way back to my apartment, ignoring the fact that we were sort of with other people. June came home an hour later with some groceries and cooked delicious beef fried rice. Looking at Oscar and June, I felt for the first time that I wasn't so alone after all. These people were my family.

At some point in the night, after we had eaten, shared a bottle of wine, and watched three episodes of

BoJack Horseman, we sat on the floor, my head on Oscar's lap. June was tweezing her eyebrows.

"Oscar, what do we think about this man that Thuy's with?"

He kept his eyes on the T.V. "Is this like an intervention?"

I laughed. "You guys are silly."

"I guess we'll just have to let her live out her ill-fated Parisian romance," June said.

Oscar didn't say anything for a whole minute. He swallowed something that he did when he got nervous or annoyed.

Closing my eyes, I promised myself that I would remember this moment. Me, Oscar, and June, three souls connected by friendship in this strange moment of our lives. None of us knew what we were doing, yet we were all very good at faking it.

It was a bit awkward at dinnertime a few days later because June couldn't make it. She had to finish the last paintings for her show this weekend. So, instead of going to our usual joint, I decided to take Oscar to the main restaurant at the Ritz.

"Oh, you're fancy," he said when we met up at the subway station.

"I just want to show my best friend the best restaurant in town," I said. "Since when did you like places like the Ritz?" he asked.

"I'd often go to places like this growing up in Vietnam. I just haven't been able to as a student living abroad."

"Hmm."

When we entered the Bar Vendome and I saw the plush red chairs and black and white photos on the walls, I immediately thought about Richard, and our time there. Was it wrong to miss something that had only existed for a couple of hours with someone who only wanted me as a toy?

"You seem a bit distracted," Oscar muttered.

"Sorry, I just had a long day at work," I said, knowing I'd done nothing the last few hours except napping.

"I feel you."

The waiter came over and asked us what we'd like to drink. Oscar asked for tap water while I ordered sparkling.

"What looks good to you?" I asked.

"Probably a steak for me. We can share it if you want." "I'll probably just get my own," I said. "If that's okay with you."

"Sure," he said.

He told me that he was going to see his cousins in the Banlieue tomorrow.

He hadn't seen them for many years.

"That's exciting," I said.

It felt awkward to be making small talk with an old friend, but then again, I wasn't quite sure what to say. I hated the fact that I wanted Richard to be here instead of Oscar. To distract myself, I asked Oscar to show me pictures of Jennifer, the girl that he was seeing. He took out his phone. She was a cute brunette with long hair and enviable bangs. Her red lipstick and strong eyeliner told me she was confident, unlike me.

"She's gorgeous," I said.

When the food came, we ate in silence.

"You know, I had a crush on you for the longest time," he said.

"Well, it sure didn't work for either of us," I said. When really, what I meant to say was, "I'm sorry I messed it up. It was the most beautiful relationship.

I've ever had."

"Yeah, we should never have dated," he said.

"It was a disaster."

We both laughed, and I took the liberty of ordering a bottle of champagne, even though it was only 5:00 o'clock on a Tuesday.

"It's on me, don't worry," I told him.

"How's your mum doing?" he asked. He, and perhaps June somewhat, were the only people who knew the extent of my tumultuous relationship with my mother. To most people, I just pretended to come from a happy, two-parent household.

"She's doing well. She's at some global women's conference."

"Impressive," he said.

"Yeah, well she did spend the last twenty years building her career instead of parenting me. So, there's that," I said, and then immediately hated myself for sounding petty.

"I feel you."

"But I guess once you turn eighteen, it's no longer okay to blame your parents for your flaws, though?"

He nodded in agreement, but then I added, "But it's easier in theory than in practice."

"Well, you can always call me when you need me," he said. "I'll always be here to listen to you talk about your most recent mother-daughter row." "Why are you such a good friend to me?" I asked.

"You remind me of myself, coming from another country and all of that.

Though you looked so out of place when we met during orientation."

"I know, the all-sweats outfit kind of gave it away."

"Yep," he said.

When the check came, much to his horror, I put down my credit card.

"Thuy!" he said. "You can't!"

"I already did," I told him. I tried to put him at ease by explaining that it was an Asian custom. He was the visitor. He seemed horrified but also grateful. He'd already told me over the phone that every single penny of his summer internship stipend was going to go to his sister's college fund.

***

Richard was back in Paris, finally, working on a new project. I invited him to Lulu White, a jazz club in Montmartre. A saxophonist and pianist father-son duo, Jean-Baptiste and Olivier Franc were playing that night.

"This guy is really good," Richard said.

I felt the thrill of being in his presence like he was gasoline to my fire. I needed him to feel alive, the thrill of not knowing when I'd get burned. It was both necessary and wrong. Long gone was the anxious little girl falling asleep in class. In Paris, with Richard, I felt closer to the kind of reality I wanted for myself. One where I felt an emotional "high" all the time. Where transgressive acts combined with the beauty of Paris made me feel alive, but I couldn't deny the feeling of home, of sweet familiarity, that Oscar had brought with him to Paris.

A poster on the wall announced that the pianist, Jean-Baptiste Franc, was the number one stride pianist in France.

"I love the saxophonist, too," I said.

I had one coconut mocktail, and Richard had a piña colada.

After the first couple of songs, June arrived with her boyfriend Louis. Oscar arrived around five minutes after them.

"*Salut les mecs,*" she said as we exchanged kisses.

I introduced the men to one another, and June gave me a mischievous look. "May the best man win," she whispered to me. "Richard, are you coming to my art opening this weekend?" June asked.

"I wouldn't miss it for the world," Richard said.

"I told him to extend his trip to Paris," I said to the group.

"Where are you based?" Oscar asked Richard.

"I travel quite a lot. I have a vineyard in Bordeaux that is my main home. However, I have projects in Dubai, Miami, and Bratislava, which means I'm

a bit all over the place."

"What kind of business?" Oscar asked.

"Wine and many other things. In Bratislava, we're working on luxury restaurants and hotels."

"Richard, I want you to take us all to your vineyard one day," I said and then realized that I sounded like a little girl pleading with her dad, which was inappropriate yet fitting, considering our age gap.

"Sure, maybe you can come to Bordeaux with me in October. Autumn is

the best time to visit, in my opinion."

"Oh, I can join from Paris," June said. She opened her cigarette case and lit a blunt. "Anybody else?"

Everyone shook their heads.

"Thuy is a very special girl," Oscar said almost out of the blue. "I'd hate to see her get hurt."

"I know our age gap may be concerning, but I care about her," Richard replied.

"I don't know if you're aware, but she's only nineteen," Oscar said.

"I know. And she is very mature for her age."

"I think that's just what older men say to justify their desire for young

women."

Meanwhile, June and I looked at each other knowingly. I felt a bit ludicrous but also amused.

"Oscar, don't be a bore," I said, gripping his arm.

Clearly annoyed, he turned to sip the wine that he'd ordered.

"Isn't this band awesome?" Richard said. Then, turning to me, he asked if I wanted a record.

"Sure," I said.

When the song was over, Richard walked up to the pianist to buy the record. "Thuy, when's your flight back to Chapel Hill?" Oscar asked me.

"I'm flying back to Vietnam next week and then back to Chapel Hill on

September 1st."

"Okay, good."

"You're ready to get rid of me, eh?"

"I just wanted to make sure everyone is doing what they're supposed to be doing. Meaning that you're staying in school."

"Okay, *dad*, thanks for the reminder. You know, this whole summer might actually be good for me. What if I need material for my future memoir?"

Richard returned to the table and handed me the record.

"Thanks, darling," I said.

"No problem," Richard replied, kissing me. "I hope I didn't miss much."

"No, you didn't do anything," June said, wistfully blowing smoke. Oscar and Richard talked a bit more about their respective work. I looked at June. It wasn't weird, was it? If your ex and your current on-and-off hook-up worked together?

"I'm a lost cause, aren't I?" I whispered to June. We'd had a lot of conversations recently about me being Richard's sort-of fling. She gave me a hug. "Sweetie, he's married. And twenty years your senior." She sighed and then continued, "You're gorgeous and will meet a million more men

like him."

"You're right, you're right," I said.

"Oscar, you're coming to my art show on Saturday! It's going to *blow you* away!"

"I'd be honored," he said.

In a whisper, I explained the phallic content of June's paintings to Oscar.

"Strap yourself in," I told him, "It might literally blow your pants off."

Throughout the night, I kept trying to watch Oscar's facial expressions.

Even if he was annoyed with Richard, he was also surprisingly calm.

Richard, on the other hand, got more handsy with me, putting his arm around my waist as if marking his territory. When Richard took a phone call, I walked out of the club with Oscar and June for a smoke. But, around 1:00 a.m., I took off with Richard while the rest of the crew went back to

June's.

****

Oscar and I went to June's art exhibit together. I showed up in a glitzy hot pink dress that emphasized my shapely hips. How strange to think that years ago, I had tried to starve myself in boarding school. Now, thanks to Kim Kardashian ripping off women of color everywhere, hips and big butts

were in style.

When June gave a short speech, I cheered her on, sipping on my glass of champagne. Instead of discussing the significance of her penis paintings, she thanked her Korean parents for instilling in her a love of seeing the world through new eyes (June's dad had moved them to Hanoi when she

was a kid).

Oscar took a picture of me with June, who wore skin-tight leather pants and a tank top that said: "Gender Freedom."

"Congrats ma chérie," I told June, who looked like she was happy but unfazed, like she had expected the crowds of people that kept on coming. Fame looked nice on her. We only had a few seconds together before she

had to run off to talk to her gallerist.

"She's a busy woman," Oscar said.

"Yes," I agreed.

Richard showed up ten minutes before the closing and made a quick round before buying the two most expensive paintings, priced at $10K each.

"I love collecting new artists' work," he said.

"Just like you collected me."

He kissed me. "You're my favorite work of art."

Richard had invited us to go to Alain Ducasse's *Le Meurice* restaurant after the opening. I'd slept over at his place the last couple of nights, knowing that he'd disappear again before I knew it. London. Singapore. Rome. I was certainly not going to be the one to pin him down. He had told me to bring my "girlfriends," but instead, I brought Oscar and June. Richard and I had dined here together not too long ago with a group of his business colleagues. I'd been the only non-model girl at the table. I'd chatted with a German model about her next Fashion Week bookings. I wondered what Richard saw in me. I thought of what my mother had once said, "If there were ten women, a man wouldn't turn away nine of them." Let's be real: I was just his flavor of the summer. I didn't care. I Googled him and found that his parents had founded an American steel company. I found photos of him, ten years younger, at a gala for New York philanthropists. His mother was a diplomat, and they had relocated to London at some point. He'd gone to Eton, then Tufts for college, then earned an M.B.A. After that, the details of his company were not as easy to find online.

"Hey, beautiful," Richard said, kissing me.

June asked him how he liked his new paintings.

"They're great." He'd bought a nude of me, my face obscured, and a painting of an odalisque enveloped in darkness.

"I thought you'd choose one of my penis paintings."

"I know, June. My office could use some large cock paintings."

June laughed. At least if my friends didn't approve of my relationship, they could approve of his sense of humor. Richard whispered in my ear, asking me what I'd like to order. I said that I was in the mood for something "seafood-y." The rest of the table agreed, then suggested that he should just order for the table. When the waitress came around, he ordered everything from corn-sauced lobster to yuzu tuna salad to squid pasta with caviar. I acted like this was just normal, but I could tell that June and Oscar were respectively impressed and annoyed. I felt the electric pull of Richard's body, his sexuality, the influence and power he held. Although I was nothing to him but the girl he was sleeping with, I felt a weird sense of affection for him. I could only attribute it to my attraction to toxic

workaholic types–my mother in masculine form. I had grown up watching her build her career from a minor bureaucrat to a powerful entrepreneur. She had important friends in different business sectors, and I often accompanied her to her dinners at their homes or in expensive hotel

restaurants.

There was less than a week before my flight back to Hanoi. In a way, I'd miss all of this. The Fantasy. The Ritz dinners and Richard and his friends and the arm candy, the people who saw money as nothing but a vehicle for lavish experiences. I had no future in Vietnam, which was its own kind of grief. Unlike my mother, I'd never felt at ease in my home country. By running away, I thought I could become famous on my own merits. I could conduct some sort of mind-blowing research and get my name in some gilded hallway of an Ivy-League university. Yet, I was quickly discovering that I was more creative and too ansty to sit in one place. It didn't help my quest to be a famed scholar that I wanted to drink wine and meet men. So far, I've accomplished both of these goals. But I read for pleasure instead of for research. I'd come to realize that I should probably be a novelist instead of a professor.

"I have known Alain since my thirties," Richard told the table.

Oscar gave me a look that said, "Really?" I squeezed his arm.

"Just enjoy dinner," I said.

"Why are we here again?" he whispered to me. I didn't have the chance to answer him before Richard started talking again. He told us that he had just returned from his trip to Dubai, where he was working on developing a condominium property. "What's the opening date looking like?" I asked him.

I wanted to ask him to take me there. Part of me hated myself for wanting to go to a place like Dubai, which I knew represented the ultimate capitalist decadence and reminded me of my own vanity. I was always trying to subdue the part of me that yearned for luxury goods. But there was another part of me that just wanted to be showered with gifts and attention. That part was not working towards her own goals, instead expecting men and other people to take care of her like a child. I did not want to be seen as shallow, but perhaps my big show of being an anti-establishment artist went out of the window the moment I linked up with Richard.

"Are you looking forward to returning to Vietnam?" Richard turned to face me while the others talked amongst themselves.

"I guess," I said. "I'll miss you." But really, I was going to miss *this*. I don't think I understood Richard the person. I saw him as the things that he was able to afford and the sexual intensity that he shared with me. I was as shallow as he was. If anything, I was grateful that this fling might be something I could write about one day. The splendor of a city that I had read about from kindergarten to the beginning of high school without knowing it. Now I knew. The Ritz and these dinners and the parties would be what I missed. Not the man. Once again, like in my childhood, money was the balm I used to treat the gaping wound inside of me. Richard smiled but withheld from returning the sentiment. Instead, he said, "You get more and more beautiful every day." "I certainly don't feel that way," I told him.

"Well, you are," he said.

My face was warm. I was a little drunk on the champagne. Richard began telling Oscar about his "early days" in investment banking. It was the only thing they had in common and could talk about. Apparently, back in his twenties, Richard worked for Morgan Stanley in London. After 30 minutes of walking down memory lane, at the end of the evening, when I left with Richard, Oscar looked hurt. And I had to admit that I got some satisfaction from that.

At Richard's place, we immediately took off our clothes and jumped into bed. I wanted to remember this forever. The sex, his body, his masculine fragrance. It would be a scent that I'd replay in my memory in the days of boredom and self-loathing ahead. Oh, how I dreaded returning to Hanoi. After sex, I got my pack of cigarettes from my purse. I returned to bed and offered him one. He shook his head.

"What will you do in Hanoi? Tell me."

What did I ever do in Hanoi? I mostly waited for the time to pass. "I don't do much, to be honest. I spend time with my family. My grandparents."

"That's good, I'm happy to hear that."

"I feel my saddest at home. It reminds me of how deeply lost and lonely I

feel all the time."

"Well, we're not meant to stay in one place forever. You'll be back in

America in no time."

"Is that why you travel so much? Do you feel that leaving places is easier than staying?"

"No, I travel because I like making money. Business ideas are always tugging at me. It's my addiction."

"And me?"

"I'm addicted to your body." He laughed.

The next morning, I woke up to find him drinking a cappuccino and reading the *Wall Street Journal*.

"You're still here?"

"Why, yes," he said.

"It's the first time I've woken up to see you in person. You're usually gone by now."

He gave me a little amused smile. I expected him to say something more, but that was all I got. I could see that the daytime. Richard was different from the nighttime Richard. Daytime, Richard was focused on work, and I was in his way. I grabbed a coffee and a croissant from the silver tray in the middle of the bed. Then I promptly put on my clothes and told him that I was leaving. He told me to keep him updated on the sale of the Toussaint paintings.

"If you get into any trouble with Sotheby's, let me know."

"Okay."

On the street, I texted Oscar, asking if he wanted to get lunch. He did not reply. Back at June's apartment, Oscar was there, and he was in a foul mood.

"What's wrong?" I asked, giving him a playful push.

"Nothing."

"Something is clearly wrong," I said, trying to lighten the mood with a laugh.

"I just feel like you're dating the wrong kind of people, Thuy. And that's not going to be good for you in the long run. Or in the short run, either."

"Fuck you. Maybe I don't want what's good for me!" I went into June's bedroom and slammed the door behind me.

"Do you still want to go for lunch?" Oscar shouted from the other side of the door.

"No!" I shouted back.

The next morning, I woke up to his email.

Email Subject: The Truth   July 15, 2016

Thuy,

You have a lot of issues. Your pattern of working excessively, writing for days nonstop at the library, followed by weeks of anxiety and depression, is, as you've told me, a pattern that began when you were a child seeing your own mother, the depressive workaholic that she was, doing the same thing. I cannot blame you for that. I have always tried to be understanding when you get yourself into some sort of self-sabotaging cycle. The day when you turned in blank pages for your paper in literary theory and had a meltdown when the professor asked if you were an ESL student. Or the day when you almost flunked a geology exam, risking your scholarship if you fell below the required GPA. Of course, you don't NEED the money the way that I do - but that's not a reason to drop out of school, especially since you've told me you don't want to return to Vietnam and be back in the same depressive, abusive environment.

Yet, I have to say that perhaps I have tolerated you and your antics slightly longer than anybody should. I've even found myself fantasizing about you and what we could be. I know you are not blind to the fact that it was not just a "very good friend" who flew out to see you in Paris on a whim in the middle of July. You know how much I hate the city and its grim ugliness, with the pickpockets and the stuck-up.

Parisians. Like a child, I had put you on a pedestal and became enamored of you! And to find you, in this vagabond state, with this thirty-nine-year-old French manchild who is using you for sex? How long is that going to last? Is this what we're going to do now - just be young and restless and waste our lives away because the whites can, and we're pretending to be like them?

But it's not just that - because I know that you're smart. So if it's not pure stupidity leading you to waste your life away here – then what? And apparently, you haven't even produced much work on your thesis. You told me that your research advisor had sent you multiple threatening emails saying that she might kick you out of her thesis class if you didn't turn in actual drafts instead of vague outlines. All of this brings me to a sad reckoning. You are a spoiled, rich, entitled, narcissistic woman who still behaves like a little girl stuck in some village in Vietnam! This baffles me, considering that your mother is one of the richest women in Hanoi, and you'd be set for life if you decided to return home. But no, you want to "prove yourself," as you've said so many times. Doing what? Playing girlfriend to old men? Just stop it.

I want you to know that the narcissism of people like you disgusts me. I wasn't always aware of it, I admit. When we first became close friends, I thought, "Hey, here's someone like me who comes from the third world and is one day going to do something amazing with their life. Sure, they have anxiety or whatever, but they're going to come around." But I was wrong. We are nothing alike. Do you know that

I've been paying college tuition for my sister and sending money home for my mom. I work three jobs. I don't even know how I was able to take two weeks off to see you in Paris. And yet, there I was. Because I love(d) you or thought I did.

If you were offended by me trying to stop you from RUINING YOUR LIFE by

attaching yourself to some old dude, thinking that it's an easier option than being a grown adult and actually taking responsibility for your life, then I'm SORRY! I'm SORRY for being there for you. I'm SORRY for thinking that you deserve more than

a half-assed life, even if it is set in this half-dead city. All this time, I was thinking that I was helping you "heal" from your traumatic childhood abuse from your narcissistic mother, who gave you plenty of money but not enough love and attention. I was wrong. You only know how to appreciate business class flights and mommy's money deposited in your account. You have no real talent. You have no real zest for

life.

But sure—I'm the "aggressive male friend"? Seriously. You need to get your shit together and stop fucking around.

Okay, that's it. I'm done. Don't bother to reply if you're just going to play the victim. But you're used to doing that, so I won't be surprised if you do.

Your friend,

Oscar.

Chapter Nine

few days later, I met up with Oscar at a cafe. We made chit-chat and ignored the giant elephant in the room. My phone began buzzing in my jacket pocket. I pulled it out and glanced at it. It was Richard. But suddenly, I felt sick of it all. Maybe Oscar was getting to me. I wanted to text Richard back and tell him it was over. I told Oscar my new revelation.

"I blocked Richard's number," I lied. "I guess, in a sense, you were right." "What?" Oscar looked incredulous.

"Well, you made your point. I had my taste of a hot French summer, and now I should just be getting on with my research," I said. "I'm just lucky to have been taken to all those fancy places."

"No," Oscar said. "He's the lucky one. He got to be in your company." "I had this fantasy of marrying Richard and moving to Paris. I wouldn't need my parents' support anymore, all the family bullshit done, and I could just live in my castle without a care in the world."

"Like Marie Antoinette?" Oscar said.

"What's wrong with that?"

I knew that a part of me was selfish, cruel, and vain. But, it was this part of

me that got me out of Vietnam, away from my muted upbringing and my

mother's cold-heartedness and vindictiveness.

"What are you going to do next?" he asked me.

"You mean, am I going back to school like a normal kid?"

"I guess," he said, laughing. "But I always thought of you as better than that.

Like you don't have to follow the traditional path we mere mortals do." "Then you mean how foolish I am to not think about my future like any normal, career-minded college student?"

"I think you'll be just fine."

He gave me a look of admiration, which instilled in me some of the confidence that I so desperately needed. Even if no one else believed in me, Oscar did.

"I feel like a bad friend for not taking you around town more. Is there anything you want to do?" I asked.

He said he wanted to go to the Musee D'Orsay and maybe the Jardin du

Luxembourg.

"Since you talked about it so much in your letters," he said.

***

The Musee D'Orsay was housed in a repurposed subway building. We walked through like two fishes swimming in an aquarium. We climbed through the stairs to the infamous *Le Dejeuner sur l'Herbe.*

"Isn't it great?" I said.

Oscar nodded.

"Why is it so famous, I wonder?"

"Anything that Manet touched is famous. But put a naked woman anywhere and…"

"I like that it is like they're situated in a mystical jungle somewhere. Even though I know it's supposed to be a public park."

I suggested that we go to a park later to recreate the scene, adding, "Jardin du Luxembourg is too prim and proper to resemble the park."

"And no naked ladies," he quipped.

We walked through the halls of the museum, neither slowly nor briskly, but at just the right pace to take a bit of everything in. I wanted to ask Oscar if he felt like a figure in a Manet painting, because I did, all the time, I felt like

time was imprinting itself on me. I was a Vietnamese woman studying in America and spending the summer in Paris, things which had felt out of reach for my Vietnamese parents but that I took for granted. What would

Manet draw if he was drawing me? Would my face resemble the woman in *A Bar at the Folies-Bergère*? Looking straight at the viewer, her face flushed, her lips pursed, the rowdy bar before her, feeling distressed but needing to stay calm for her job. I had read somewhere that Manet encouraged his students to follow their intuition and paint what they wanted rather than what was fashionable according to the artistic conventions of the time.

"I approve," Oscar said. "So much art nowadays feels stifled to me." "I think that authenticity is a trap, though," I said. "One moment, you feel authentic, and the next, you feel like a terrible fraud."

"Is that what you think life is? An endless search for authenticity?" he asked. "I'm not sure. The more I search for authenticity, the less it seems to come.

Mostly, I just try to be me, however flawed I am," I said.

We were now strolling through the Monet gallery, and I told Oscar that I got bored by the endless water lilies, which seemed to slightly offend him.

"You're just being a contrarian. I think they're great."

We grabbed a bite to eat nearby. A nice cheesy croque monsieur for me and a steak and pomme frites for Oscar. The next day, he'd be on his flight back to New York.

"Excited for New York?" I asked.

"No," he said. "It'll just be work and more work."

"Do you ever miss Senegal?"

"All the time," he said. "It features heavily in my dreams. The food, the smells. Mostly the smell of water, if you can believe it. The water there has a certain fragrance." He asked me what I thought about when I thought about home.

"Destruction. But also my mom's cooking, which is probably the one way she authentically communicated love for me."

"Do you think that's what our lives will always be about? Missing our homelands everywhere we go, no matter how much we wanted to get away

in the first place?"

"I guess so."

"I find the paradox of the homesickness was the most difficult thing about living as an expat."

***

"I'll miss you," I said to Oscar, kissing him on the cheek. He had come to June's apartment to say goodbye. He would stay with his cousins before flying back to the States.

"You sure about that?" he said. "After all that I said in that email?"

"Of course, you're one of my best friends."

He sighed and then gave me a very long look at me.

"You need to take care of yourself, okay?"

"I will, don't you worry."

After he left, I collapsed on the sofa and fell into a deep sleep. When June came home from the studio, it was nighttime. I had been asleep for hours.

She turned on a light. I sat up and rubbed my eyes.

"You okay?" she asked, sitting down next to me.

"Yeah."

"You still love him, huh?"

"Yes."

"Well, what about Richard?"

"I love him too. But just the *idea* of him." We looked at each other and started laughing.

"I'm a mess," I said to her, shaking my head.

"Maybe what you feel for them is what you should be giving yourself. I'm going to take a shower," she said abruptly and then went to the bathroom.

***

The next day, I went to Emilie's studio. We had managed to secure a meeting with the head of Southeast Asian paintings at Sotheby's, and we were going there with the knowledge that her father's paintings were worth at least ten times what they proposed. I was going to be the one negotiating the Nhat Toussaint prices. If they didn't give us a fair offer, we might have to go somewhere else. Or we could take up Richard on his offer and be represented by his gallery. But something in my chest told me I did not want that to happen. I felt that Richard was tempestuous love, and that that should be separated from art, my work, which was a pure love.

At the meeting, the director of Sotheby's Paris showed up looking like Jean.

Gabin in *Touchez pas Au grisbi*. He had with him the head of the Southeast Asian painting department, who looked like an accountant. I greeted them warmly. *"Bonjour*, I am Thuy Nguyen, and this is Emilie Toussaint, daughter of Nhat Toussaint."

The two men both gave us weird, condescending looks, scanning us up and down.

"We want to talk about the proposed prices for Nhat's paintings," I said.

"What about them?" the accountant asked, not very kindly.

"I don't understand," the other one interjected. "We've already sent Ms.

Emilie, the terms."

"*Monsieur*, your proposal greatly undervalues my client's father's oeuvre. These paintings have been valued elsewhere at triple, even quadruple those numbers. Here is our counter to your proposal." I handed him the document. Emilie sat next to me, and she seemed rattled. She had walked this path before, and it had ended poorly. The head of the Southeast Asian painting department flipped through the first couple of pages of our proposal and shook his head disapprovingly. He passed it to his partner, who mumbled something along the lines of "Impossible!" Then they told us that they couldn't approve of our proposal but that their original offer remained until the end of the year.

Standing outside the building, waiting for a taxi, I noticed that Emilie seemed distant; she had been disappointed one too many times.

"Emilie, don't worry," I said. "I'll fight this. I'll ask around for help. It's not right what they're doing."

"It's all right, sweetheart," she said. "Everything in due time."

Maybe I was in over my head. I thought about how all the hard work Emilie and I had done was not paying off. Then my mind flashed to the terrible dinner with Richard and Oscar, how confused I was about love, and just how generally messed up everything was. I felt lost and began to weep.

"Oh honey, what's wrong?" Emilie asked.

"It just feels so unfair."

"Life's unfair," she said. "But that doesn't mean that we can't do anything about it. Sometimes, things work out, even when we don't see the way forward."

Wiping my eyes with the sleeves of my shirt, I took a deep breath to calm myself down.

"Now, let's go get lunch, shall we?"

I nodded. I felt like a good ham and cheese crêpe would surely fix all of my troubles.

That night, I got Richard to agree to represent the Nhat Toussaint Estate.

With two days left before my flight to Hanoi, I went into a frenzy and finished chapters three through five of my grant paper like a madwoman. I had been fickle and procrastinating, but now I went into obsessive mode, unearthing everything I could find about Nhat Toussaint and his time in

Paris. I wrote chapters on the French painters that he admired and emulated, and on the Vietnamese and Western philosophies he was working from.

Shortly after finishing the last word of the last chapter, I called Richard. He picked up immediately, his voice warm.

"Hello, beautiful."

"Hi, Richard," I said.

I told him that I was thinking about him and wondering if he was still in town and how I wanted to see him before I left.

"Where are you?" he asked. He was only going to be in Paris for the next twenty-four hours.

"I'm at June's. 20th arrondissement."

"Send me your address."

June was out for the night with some girlfriends. When Richard finally came to the apartment, he immediately ripped off my clothes. We fucked in the living room, then shared a postcoital cigarette. He then told me to put on some clothes so he could take me out. We'd gone to fancy dinners at the restaurants of five-star hotels, but tonight, he was bringing me to a nightclub. Le Soirée had an all-black marble façade. The marble, Richard told me, was imported from Greece with a tint of opal blue, looking like a transparent painting of the Mediterranean Sea. As we walked past the long line of twenty-somethings and well-dressed older couples, he explained to me that he knew the owner of the club.

"Welcome back, Mr. H," the bouncer said.

There was a cage hanging from the ceiling where female dancers, naked except for their glittering bras and panties, moved their bodies slowly and sensually as if they had been drugged. Some people were dressed in costumes, but most of the attendees were just like us, costumeless, except for the guises we all wore to obscure our unrealized identities. I presumed that those who were dressed up in costumes—flamingo plumes, beer maids, a large poodle—were also working at the club as either waiters or paid partygoers.

We sat down at a table in the back with a good view of the crowd. The music was so loud I wondered how long I could stand it. Richard produced a small vial from his pocket and asked me if I wanted any blow. He put some on his thumb and held it out to me, and I snorted it up. It went down my throat like a small, pleasant snake. "Now you can drink without getting drunk," he said. It was like he had given me the keys to the kingdom of heaven.

What happened next was a blur. Innumerable sources of light, white powder, and a hot liquid, which I later realized was alcohol. Richard was doing more and more cocaine, his hands all over me like an octopus. I danced for hours. Moving my body to the freedom of the night. I don't think Richard was on the dance floor, but other figures around me were collapsing into one another. I got lost in a trance; I saw the moment I came out of my mother's womb. I remembered the night I decided I hated her. I remembered the emotions that I'd felt all my life – hatred, anger, fear, and then suddenly, they all melted into love, calm, and joy. I wanted joy more than anything. I realized I didn't know where Richard was. Was I alone? I didn't care. I didn't care about anything. I would always be in Paris in my mind. Paris in my mind. I wanted to live, yet I also wanted to die. The world was full of meaning, but I didn't care to understand much of it. I wanted the world to be lost from meaning so I could emerge as nothing at all. The black hole of despair that resided in my heart went away. I was free from it.

"Wake up, wake up," June said, pushing my plane ticket into my hand. "You have a flight to catch."

Chapter Ten

Hanoi, mid-August, 2015

When I arrived in Hanoi, still hungover from my final night in Paris, the torrents of motorbikes flying by my car made me feel ill at ease. The driver, Dung, was the distant son of a distant great aunt's sister. He had been with our family for the last fifteen years, had taken my suitcases and put them in the trunk. I first met him when I was ten. He had driven me to school every morning in grade school. Though he was only six years older than me, he already had a three-year-old boy. He had come from my mother's side of the family. "How are your wife and kid, *em*?"

"Both are doing good, thank you," he said, glancing at me in the rearview mirror. "You look good; looks like you've lost some weight," he said.

"I just have a skinny face," I told him.

In the rearview mirror, I saw my reflection. I looked as white as a ghost.

Good, because coming back to Hanoi made me feel like a ghost. We arrived at our apartment building. In the early 2000s, my dad bought this plot, which was practically only marsh land. He and my mother spent about five years laying a foundation and then building a ten-story apartment building. We lived on the ninth and tenth floors.

Dung carried my suitcases to the elevator, and we rode up to the ninth floor. I knocked on the door, but it was already open.

"Hello, sweetheart," Mom said, smiling like the graceful mother that she was half of the time. I loved her so much in those moments, and it made me forget about the other times. We exchanged pleasantries about the flight and drove here.

"I got you some things from Paris," I said, pulling out the scarf that I had found for her in a vintage market from my bag.

"How nice of you," she said. I felt happy to be able to give her something, even though I'd used her credit card to buy it.

"I'm sure you'll wear this instead of your designer scarves," I teased.   "No, I love it. I don't want to wear too many designer names. These days, it's a bit tacky, don't you think?"

I smiled. This was the closest we ever got. Things we bought, gifts we exchanged. Things defined our relationship in a way touch never could. I could not remember the last time she'd given me an actual hug, although she sometimes still held my hand when we crossed the street.

"You look pale, honey," she said. "You must be tired. You should go take a nap."

I nodded.

"Where's dad?"

"He's in his study downstairs. He'll come up soon."

"Where Harry?"

"At his after-school English class. You really should get some sleep. Your cousins and aunts and uncles are coming for dinner in an hour."

"Okay, Mom."

"And maybe take a shower too, after."

"I will."

In my bedroom, I was flooded with a sense of smallness. The smallness of childhood is defined by the pink wallpaper and green curtains patterned with drawings of Mario, Princess Peach, and random animals. There was my twin-size trundle bed I used for sleepovers. I missed those days. Sometimes, I wondered why I wanted to go abroad so badly when so many good memories were also here. The mom who cooked, the friends who slept over, our home. But of course, there was another side to Mom. I was past the stage of being naively hopeful. But I could at least be grateful for the

good moments.

Mom was preparing one of her typical big dinners. As the most successful member of the family on both her side and my father's side, it was always a big party when she hosted. The single female cousins came slightly early to help with the cooking. I went into the kitchen and saw at least eight dishes being prepared. Since the war, it was typical for my family to celebrate with lots of food because the elders were still traumatized by times when there had been much less. Seeing my cousins, who I'd grown up with, made me swell with joy. "Look who it is!" Min exclaimed as she gave me a hug. Even though she had suffered the most out of all the cousins, she was the happiest. Her father had left her mother because she couldn't give him a son after birthing two girls. So, Min and her sister grew up in comparably modest circumstances. Yet they never lacked affection. That made my interaction with Min bittersweet. I had more things than her, went to better vacation spots, and ate at better restaurants. But I had never seen Min's mom, Auntie Susu, treat Min with the kind of contempt that my mom often demonstrated towards me.

In our home, everybody orbited around Mom, whether they were cousins, half the age of Mom, an elder, or one of Mom's nine siblings. She had been born in the year of the tiger and had the energy of a tiger. Dinner was all the familiar traditional Vietnamese dishes with a few twists. Baked lobster with cheese, papaya salad with lime, boiled chicken with fish sauce, and *rau muong*. I begrudgingly asked Mom and the other women if they needed help; it was an empty gesture, and everyone knew it. They laughed and sent me on my way. Growing up, I'd never had to do any cooking or other chores. My parents wanted me to study and succeed. Plus, my family always had a live-in maid who prepared lunch and dinner. Tina, our maid, had come to town from the countryside when she was in her early thirties after her husband had divorced her. Her two daughters were eleven and fifteen.

The girls called Mom *bà* for grandma and me *cô* for auntie.

Because Mom was one of ten, she had many nieces and nephews. I hung out and chatted with the fifteen or so cousins while the meal was being prepared. They all seemed so happy; I rarely saw such natural joy and conviviality in the west. Everyone, even the elderly, spoke to me with affection because I was my mother's daughter and because they benefited from my mother and her wealth. She'd many of my cousins, on both sides of the family, get some sort of job or opportunity.

During dinner, the men smoked and both the men and women drank. I watched Mom joke with her family members. I admired her for being the glue that held the family together. In many ways, this was a good life, better than life in the west. My dad was a contemplative man, and he did not say much during the dinner, observing everything and serenely eating the dishes placed before him. He was a scientist and, therefore, saw the world according to logic. When he'd lived in the Soviet Union, he had earned a degree in meteorology and geology, an interesting choice for a boy from Ninh-Binh. It was there that he'd met and married my mother. When they returned to Hanoi together, he worked in the local meteorology department, but he quit when Mom began working full-time. Mom was gone so much, and he wanted to be home for my brother and me. He was basically a stay-at-home dad. I think he would have preferred to have stayed in academia. Though he never said it outright, the need to provide stability for the family may have kept him from a breakthrough in his research. It had been his lifelong wish that me or my brother would continue where he'd left off.

After dinner, Min drove me to get bubble tea. I chose brown sugar milk tea, and Min got apricot tea. As we sipped our drinks, I asked her about China. She had lived there for a couple of months, going to a trade school to teach Russian and working as a waitress.

"It was good. I had a job at a small Chinese business translation firm."

"But you no longer work there?"

"No, I'm selling things on Facebook. It allows me to have a flexible schedule."

Min had always had plans to go abroad, mostly to learn languages and then work on the side. Unlike me, her family didn't have a lot of money. Her mom couldn't wire her money to go to Paris and fuck around.

The next morning, my mother asked me if I wanted to go shopping. Shopping together was something my mother and I always did when I visited. She would take me to expensive stores I couldn't afford on my own. But designer clothes were not my style. I didn't really want to go shopping, yet I wanted to go because it was the only time I'd be able to experience a sense of closeness with my mom. At Louis Vuitton, Mom picked out a navy bag in their signature motif. I had wide straps and thick leather binding. I thought it was ugly, but I didn't want to upset her, so I kept my mouth shut. The last time I'd said no, she threw a huge fit and walked out of the store.

"What do you think?" Mom said.

"Hmm, it's interesting for sure," I said.

"Do you not like it?"

My face belied my emotions; I couldn't hide sadness or joy from her. But it didn't matter. Mom didn't care about my emotions. My sadness repulsed

her. "I think you should get it. It's certainly nicer than the ugly clothes you pick out for yourself all the time," she said. We continued to look at handbags. On another counter, I saw a pink bag with a magnet opening. I thought it was classy, unlike the navy one.

"Can I see that one?" I asked the shop assistant.

The assistant brought over the bag, and I felt the giddiness that only an expensive handbag could bring me. But I knew the feeling wouldn't last.

"So ugly," Mom said. She told me that the bag she had picked was better.

And since she was the one paying, there was no arguing.

I used to try to defend my opinions. But only one person could be right in this relationship. I didn't want to challenge her. And besides, it didn't really matter. For dinner, we were going to the new Marriott restaurant. I put on a skintight bespoke navy dress that I'd bought in Paris. Mom brusquely told

me to take it off.

"Don't you know you look fat in that dress?"

I complied. Even though I burned with anger, I didn't want to fight her. In the car, Mom went on and on about her great day. Her meetings had gone well, and she would be able to sell more pharmaceuticals next year. Blah, blah, blah. I wanted to scream, "Shut the fuck up!"

At the restaurant, we ordered a dim sum. "How are you doing?" I asked Harry. My brother was quiet, and I was the one who usually started the conversation between us. When I left for boarding school, I worried about him. I knew that left to his own devices, he'd be on his phone or playing video games day and night. And he was mostly left to his own devices. "Hey, what do we think about going on vacation while you're here? Maybe Nha Trang or Da Nang." Mom said.

"Let's do Da Nang," I said, trying to muster some enthusiasm.

Dad simply nodded, and Harry was back on his phone.

"Thuy, you book the hotel when we get home. A room for me and you. One for your brother and dad."

"Sure, mom."

The dinner went smoothly. Between planning the vacation and enjoying the delicious food, it almost felt pleasant. Mornings in Hanoi always made me feel at peace. Even though there were loud motorbikes and the rush of the morning commute began at seven, I loved everything about the smoggy air, the breakfast foods at the neighborhood cafes, and the quiet footsteps of Tina making us tea. But by the afternoon, I had already got myself into a kerfuffle with my mother over something stupid. I was sitting on the couch, looking at nothing, doing nothing, when out of nowhere, she attacked me.

"Why do you always act like a victim?" she said.

"What?"

"I know there's a pit of sadness in you, and I don't know why."

"I'm just sitting here."

"No, you're not just sitting there."

There were a mere two weeks left before I returned to Chapel Hill. I'd had the idea that perhaps, on this trip, she and I could come to some sort of understanding with each other. That she would see that I was an adult now and that I had already accomplished quite a lot. On my own. Like she had, it was delusional, but it was perhaps what I wanted more than anything: equilibrium between us. But for now, I just wanted to stop looking at her.

Because being around her was terribly upsetting.

I found Dad in the living room watching television.

"Hi, Dad."

"Hey."

I sat next to him on the couch and held his hand, then put my head on his shoulder. Dad was a steady presence growing up. Not that we talked much, but he took care of me, keeping up with my school reports and doctor visits. The memories of him taking me out for pho or banh mi after school were my favorite memories from growing up.

The Napper

My dad was watching a National Geographic documentary about Cat Ba langurs, an endangered primate found in the Cat Ba archipelago.

"Thuy, do you remember when we visited the Cat Ba archipelago?"

"Yes, but I don't remember seeing this animal."

"They're diurnal. They stay in sleeping caves and ledges to avoid predators and extreme weather."

"Relatable," I said, wondering if my napping was how I protected myself from imaginary predators. A part of me wished that I could stay here forever, just like this, ensconced in my father's care.

Later that night, we had over a group of my mom's friends from her women's business association. There was Auntie Kim, who owned a group of private hospitals in Hanoi; Auntie Lien, who worked as the secretary to the Communist Party of Hanoi; and Auntie An, who owned over a hundred clothing factories. They were each powerful in their own way, and when they got together, they resembled a *Rich Housewives* cast in the way they amused themselves and bitched about their families. I often wondered if my mother actually belonged. Yes, we were comfortable, but Mom still worried about money. She told me that she'd put in sweat and tears to be in a leadership position at her pharmaceutical company, but she wasn't the sole owner.

As Tina served the dishes that Mom had carefully selected—fried scallop spring rolls, papaya salad, Da Nang summer rolls with thick fish sauce paste--I watched the women. They were the highest example of Vietnamese womanhood, so strong and successful. Unbreakable. What did I have to offer in comparison? Would I and others from the Western "brain leakage" generation end up being slaves to Western capitalism? Sometimes, I wondered if it would have been better if I had stayed in the Vietnamese education system or returned to the country after high school. I could have worked at my mom's company and made decent money and afforded everything Hanoi had to offer. But the Western world was calling me. Because I had left here when I was fourteen, when I returned, I felt like a perpetual child, unable to talk like an adult in Vietnamese. I was overly polite and felt like I was perpetually translating in my head. Sadly, I could only communicate like an adult in English.

"Thuy," Auntie Kim said, "you have to meet my son, Andy. He was a math major at MIT."

"Oh really? What a smart boy," Mom remarked. "Thuy, you guys have to exchange numbers."

"Sure," I mumbled.

"Make sure to remind me after dinner, honey," Auntie Kim said.

"First, shouldn't we ask if she has a boyfriend?" Auntie Lien said. "Oh, Thuy is busy studying," Mom said. "She doesn't have time to talk to boys."

I did my best to keep a neutral face. But I felt like a fraud. I'd slept with at least five men this past year.

"Thuy is so smart. She's on a full scholarship," my mother said, and her friends oohed and ahh-ed.

The food was mind-numbingly good. The one thing that kept me sane when I was home was the food. I would watch Mom cooking dinner for us, which she managed to do most nights. She didn't know what was going on in my day, in my life, or in my head, but she made sure she kept me supremely well-fed.

"How is the politburo these days?" Auntie An asked Auntie Lien.

"You know, ladies, it's getting spicier. There's talk that the president's party might be under investigation soon."

"I heard," Mom said. "What a shame. They're going after everybody now." "Yes, the Party Secretary is going to try to first go after the president's men, then eventually the president himself."

I helped Tina pour more beer into the women's glasses. There was a lot more political talk, which I couldn't follow. I only knew that somebody was going to be stabbed in the back and that it was no joke.

After dinner, Mom called me aside.

"Don't talk so fast when my friends talk to you. You sound like the help." "Yes, Mom."

"And stand up straight. Why do you always have your back hunched like that?"

"Yes, Mom."

I played a video game with Harry for a while before going to bed. There was something so pure and joyful about being with him that it almost made coming home worth it. After hanging out with Harry, I stayed up a while looking at the ceiling and then, unable to sleep, I watched some Mukbang YouTube videos. Watching thin and pretty Asian women gorge on food was a secret guilty pastime of mine. If I could, I would gorge myself and never stop.

***

Mom was at work, and Dad was in his office, so I decided to go to Hanoi.

The Napper

Lotte Mall with Min. Min's presence was like a comforting hug to me. She was a stark contrast to Mom, always treating me with warmth and affection. When we were kids, Min would try to defend me when I got into trouble with Mom. Because Min's father wasn't around, Mom acted like a second mom to her, and Mom would back off a little from being so mean to me when Min was around. We went to the arcade on the fifth floor of the mall. Even though I felt slightly old for the arcade, Min said it would be fun, so I went with it. Although Min was five years older than me, she felt younger. We started with one of the shooting alien games. Min was laughing and smiling, and I couldn't help but momentarily forget the stress of staying with my parents.

I wondered if the reason why Min's energy felt so light and joyful was because she didn't have a Mom like mine. Min's mom, Auntie Susu, who'd been a Buddhist nun for the last five years, never once treated her with anger or disdain, at least not that I'd ever witnessed. Silently, I wished that we could trade mothers. I'd happily choose a simpler life, one without the Hanoi penthouse, the boarding school, or the international trips, in return for feeling an ounce closer to my mother.

After the alien game, we went to the dance game and danced to some Japanese anime music. I was quick on my feet, but Min got frazzled by the quick speed and tripped.

"Ha ha, you fell!" I taunted.

"What kind of song is this anyway?" she said, laughing and brushing off her pants.

Notwithstanding all the parents accompanying their kids, we were the oldest people on the floor. I thought some more about my childhood and the time I spent with my extended family, many of whom didn't have much in terms of material things. These were my most peaceful memories. That was something that I resented Mom for. Her behavior had pushed me to leave Vietnam, which had separated me from my extended family. I hated her for that.

"How's the Facebook shop going?" I asked Min.

"It's so-so, you know."

"How much do you make?" That question would be a faux pas in the Western world, but in Vietnam, it was an acceptable question among friends and family.

"Enough to go out and buy food," she said, laughing.

Unlike my mom, her mom didn't help her out financially. That realization made me feel guilty for being angry with Mom. I was a spoiled, ungrateful brat. Why couldn't I be grateful for my mother's hard work? We left the arcade to the window shop. Most Hanoians didn't actually shop at the international malls because the prices were super inflated, but it was fun to walk around. In the clothing stores, the largest size was the equivalent of a U.S. medium. I felt slightly self-conscious about my body, which was larger than the average woman here. "These clothes are too small for me."

"What are you talking about? You're so skinny; what are you talking about?" Min replied. I immediately felt bad for complaining about my weight, knowing that Min was ten or fifteen pounds overweight. She looked bigger than she was because she carried weight in her tummy, which I didn't.

"Mom said I look fat," I said.

Min laughed. "Don't mind what she says."

While we walked, we held hands, and I was reminded of why I often felt isolated in the States. The most obvious reason, of course, was that none of my close family members were abroad. In the U.S., I didn't have Min to hold my hand on a Wednesday in the mall. I didn't have anybody to show me how to have silly fun or reassure me that I wasn't as bad as I thought I was. Once we were finished with the mall, we got on Min's scooter. Another advantage of having many cousins was that they always drove me around.

"Do you want to have lunch with my mom?" Min asked.

"Sure."

She drove us back to the small, ground-floor apartment that she shared with Auntie Susu. "My dear Thuy," Auntie Susu said, hugging me. She was wearing her gray nun cloak. I could feel her bony rib cage during our embrace. She had lost even more weight since the last time I'd seen her.

"Auntie, you are so skinny," I said.

"It's the new diet that Mom's been on," Min said. "She's even cut out vegetables, so now it's just purple rice and sesame seeds."

"Is that enough to stay alive?" I said, dumbfounded.

"Mom's new Buddhist master even told her to cut down on water as much as possible!" Min said, annoyed.

"Really?"

Auntie Susu laughed and brushed it off, saying that the diet had been researched. "Look at me; isn't this the healthiest I've ever looked?" Later on, when we were alone, Min whispered in my ear that my

Mom and Min were plotting to undo the hold Auntie Susu's Zen master had on her.

"We're afraid she might be in a cult," Min told me.

"My goodness."

The three of us had lunch together. While Auntie Susu munched on said purple rice and sesame seeds, Min and I had a normal meal of white rice, a soy sauce omelet, and sautéed spinach. Because I was a "special guest," Auntie Susu also brought out a plate of little salted shrimp. They tasted divine with the rice.

When I got back home, Mom asked me how my day was. I told her about hanging out with Min and Auntie Susu. Mom seemed to be happy hearing that I was hanging out with her side of the family.

"Auntie Susu has lost a lot of weight," I told Mom.

"Yeah, it's the cult she's in. That wacky Buddhist priest insists on not even drinking water! Doesn't she know that actual priests eat meat now and then? The last time I met the head of a temple, he offered our party steamed shrimp, and then he ate most of it! I'll take you to the temple soon, though.

You haven't been since you got home, and that's not good."

"Right."

"Now that I'm thinking about it, would you mind going up to the prayer room and lighting an incense stick? Thank the ancestors for bringing you home safely."

I nodded my consent.

Upstairs, in our prayer room, I took three sticks from the cupboard. In front of me was the gigantic wooden offering table flanked on either side by smaller tables. On each table was a photograph of a passed ancestor. On the middle table was my great-grandfather; on the right table, my father's youngest brother, who had died shortly after the Vietnam War from a brain hemorrhage; and on the left table, my maternal grandmother. Usually, when we prayed on the big Buddhist dates, we prayed as a family. On those occasions, Mom or Dad would read the official chant from a book of Buddhist chants. When I prayed alone, I went straight for the facts. "Dear ancestors, thank you for safely guiding me home. Thank you for protecting me. Please protect the health of my mom, my dad, my brother, and me."

Then I bowed three times, as was the custom.

After dinner, I went to my room and checked my phone. A text from Oscar:

"FaceTime?"

"Okay," I replied.

His face on the screen looked nerdier than it did in real life, his thick, black-framed glasses taking up much of the video frame.

"How's it going?" I asked him.

"All good, all good. Back in New York now," he replied, turning the camera to the room. It was a small, unremarkable room with a bed, a desk covered in programming books, and a chair.

"Wanna see my room?" I said, turning my camera around.

"That's a lot of pink teddy bears and green lollipops on your curtains," he remarked, chuckling.

"I know, right?"

"What else is going on with you?"

"Well, things with Mom haven't been as bad as I thought."

"That's great!" he said.

"And you? What's new in the world of technology and banking?"

"Just a lot of work. I'll be busting my ass the first few years before getting even an inch of a break."

"LOL!"

"Vietnam looks fun. I saw all the food pics you posted on IG."

"Yeah, the food is incredible."

There was a moment of silence where we just stared at each other and smiled. I felt comforted by his presence, and I could tell that he did by mine.

"Have you had any time to do fun things?" I asked him.

"I watch a lot of movies. I just watched *Eternal Sunshine of the Spotless Mind.*"

"What's that about?"

"You should watch it. It's about a breakup. Instead of losing his mind missing her, the boyfriend goes to a scientist to have his memories of her deleted. But then he instantly regrets it. He wants her back in his life after all."

"That's so stupid. Why doesn't he just get a new girlfriend?"

"Cause they were MEANT to be together."

I laughed, but I also wondered if Oscar and I meant to be together in some alternate version of time and space.

"I don't know if I'm ready to go back to Chapel Hill. The idea of three more years is just depressing. Especially without you," I told Oscar.

"You'll have so many fun experiences," he said. "Next year will be even better than the last. It always goes like that."

"Not for me. I'm excited to nap, though. It's hard to get a good one in around here."

"Have you talked to Richard at all?"

"No," I said, laughing. "We both knew it was never going to amount to anything. It was just a Parisian fling." Just saying that made me feel a bit of pain, and a part of me flinched from the inside. I didn't think it would hurt to part from a hook-up, but because I had cared about Richard, it still hurt.

"Just like I was your Chapel Hill fling?"

"You were definitely more than a fling, dude."

"Well, so were you."

"Thank you very much."

The call ended. I stared at my ceiling. I missed Oscar deeply. A part of me was terrified to go back to Chapel Hill without him. Another part felt that it was good that he wouldn't be there as a crutch for me to grip onto. Mom knocked on my door.

"Here's some cut fruit." A beautiful plate of orange slices gleamed at me.

"Oh, thanks, Mom."

"Who were you talking to?"

"Just a friend."

"Hmm."

After she left, I spent some time fleshing out my thoughts on paper. I wanted to figure out my emotional pull towards Oscar. It was strong, but we'd be living in separate cities now. Plus, I was the one who'd broken up with him. Guilty as charged. I wondered if there was still a chance. I knew from the look in his eyes that he still felt strongly about me. A crazy thought popped into my head. What if I were to surprise him in New York in the fall? Pulling up flights on the computer, I saw the cheapest roundtrip flight from Durham to JFK was $299 in mid-October. Who knows—maybe this would be my chance to fix everything.

Chapter Eleven

In the middle of the night, I heard loud sounds coming from my parent's bedroom. It wasn't quite a scream, more like a loud grunt. Dad was away in the countryside. I was surprised that Mom was awake this late, but she was a social media addict and often scrolled Facebook and Instagram late into the night. I knocked on their door.

"Mom, are you okay?"

Nobody answered. I paused outside their bedroom. After almost five years living abroad, I'd become accustomed to minding nobody's business but my own, and I didn't want to infringe on her space. But something told me to go in and check on her. When I opened the door, Mom was sitting on the far end of the bed, facing the windows. She was mumbling something, and the mumbling quickly turned into plaintive whimpering.

Then, she clearly enunciated, "Mom, are you okay?"

There was nobody there but me, but she definitely wasn't talking to me. She stood up and walked a few paces with her arms outstretched.

"Are they feeding you good food there? I sent you so much food and cash to buy anything you want." She fell to her knees. "Mommy, I'm so sorry… I'm sorry you didn't get to stay long enough to see what we've built. We have a big house now. We're not living dirty and poor anymore. I told myself I'd get you set up and comfortable, but you had to leave early. Mummy, I feel so guilty."

Then she began screaming gibberish in no discernable language, which turned into pure rage. Tears were streaming down her face. I rushed over to where she was and wrapped my arms around her.

"Mummy, wake up," I said, brushing her tears away with my fingers.

Abruptly, she came to. "What? What happened?"

"You just had a bad dream, Mom."

Calming down, she said, "Oh, it wasn't a dream." I had never seen her like this before, so frail and scared. "Grandma came. She came back from the dead to talk to me. I think she knew that I was feeling sad that she left us so soon. Especially since I could take care of her now."

I held her by the shoulders and guided her back into bed. I lay her down and pulled the covers over her. She took my hand and stared at me. Her face reminded me of a picture of my grandmother that I'd seen in our family album ages ago: she had sharp eyes that could just as easily be fierce or kind. Seeing my mom like this, this usually strong woman as vulnerable as a child, caused me to feel love and care for her. She quickly fell back asleep. She looked peaceful and beautiful. There was a yellow aura around her. I sat by her side for a long while. The room was quiet. I thought, you grow up, and you have your list of grievances against your parents, and then one day you realize that the role of parent and child could easily be reversed. She opened her eyes and started speaking to me, her voice calm. I couldn't tell if she was talking in her sleep, but she didn't sound how she normally sounded. "Grandma looked pretty. She was wearing the clothes I sent her." Mom was referring to the designer clothes made of paper that we burned during Buddhist ceremonies. "Grandma told me that I needed to go to the graveyard more often to tend to her grave. I called our cousins in the country to fix it, but she's telling me it's still very dirty."

When it seemed that she'd finally fallen into a deep sleep, I got up to go back to bed. When I reached the door, she said, "I miss you all the time." I turned around and said, "I miss you too, Mom," We looked at each other for a minute, recognizing our deep bond. Finally, I said, "Go to sleep now, Mom." And then I left the room.

Back in my bed, I had trouble falling asleep. I felt the urge to write in my journal about what had just happened. The story of a mother grieving her own mother. And of the mother's daughter walking in on her mother talking to a ghost. Every woman would inevitably feel that we'd let down our ancestors in some way. Leaving one's family was the biggest offense of all. And yet, I was so readily committing that great moral transgression without even blinking an eye.

Chapter Twelve

Three Months Later, New York, Fall 2015

Upon landing at JFK with my overfilled baby pink carry-on, I waited at the baggage claim. It felt strange to finally reunite with Oscar. I'd be spending Thanksgiving break with him. I saw his silhouette approaching me. There was my friend, my former lover, his lanky frame replaced with defined muscles. He'd grown a thin mustache, which complimented his signature black glasses. "It's been too long," I told him as he hugged me. I breathed in his cologne, a pleasant smell of sandalwood and cardamom.

"Too, too long," he said before picking up my bags. He told me to wait there while he went to get his car. A few minutes later, he pulled up in an old, dark blue Camry.

"How long have you had this car?" I asked him.

"For almost five months now. My uncle sold it to me for very cheap." "It must be nice to have a car in New York. I love the subway, but it can get congested sometimes."

"Yeah, I still take the subway to work, though and use my cars for shopping, et cetera," he said.

As he drove me back to his place in Bed Stuy, I thought about when we first met at Chapel Hill and where we were now. Of course, I was only one year wiser from the little girl who'd lost her virginity as a freshman, then spent a summer frolicking about Paris while he was now a grown man starting a career in Manhattan. He looked a lot older than the last time I'd seen him, only a few months ago.

"How's work these days? Last time we talked, you mentioned how you'd started to feel like it wasn't the best fit."

"Well, I'm definitely overworked, but it's not the overworking that bothers me. I think I'm just genuinely not interested in computer engineering, although I need the money."

"You should do what makes you happy," I said.

"Well, *c'est la vie*."

"C'est la vie," I repeated. I felt slightly worried hearing that he wasn't following his passion. Then suddenly, I realized that even after knowing him all this time, I still wasn't quite sure what exactly he was passionate about.

As we drove through the tunnel towards Brooklyn, a breeze must have caught, and outside the tunnel, the yellow autumn leaves started to pepper the streets, leaving a golden trail. I felt my heart warm at the sight of the brownstones, a charming, quintessential New York sight.

We arrived at his apartment. It was through a little iron gate, then down some stairs to the garden apartment. In the foyer was a large painting of Paris. The painting showed a couple looking at the outdoor book stalls by the Seine.

"How cute!" I exclaimed.

"I saw it on Etsy and thought of this summer," he said earnestly.

I blushed a little, and my heart felt warmed by his affection. It was apparent that the trip was of great significance to him. I sat down on his sofa and kicked off my shoes. "Coffee?" he asked. I nodded, "Yes, please." He went to the kitchen and made me a stovetop espresso, then sat down next to me on the couch.

"Thanks," I said, sipping the coffee.

He reached over and took hold of my hand. Did he still have feelings for me? I shook my head. Get it together, Thuy. Don't imagine things that aren't there any longer. Holding hands didn't have to be weird or overly suggestive; in Vietnam, friends held hands all the time. So perhaps he was just being affectionate because he missed me.

"I have the evening all planned out for you," he said.

"That's sweet," I replied.

"We'll start by going to the Strand and Union Square, then get ramen, and then, if you're feeling up to it, we can catch a movie at Film Forum." "Sounds good to me," I said, taking a big sip of my coffee. But I knew full well that no matter how much coffee I drank, I'd most likely need to squeeze in a nap between now and the end of the day.

Before we left the apartment, Oscar had to grab some of his stuff from his bedroom so I got to take a glimpse of his space. There were posters of *Kill Bill* and The Beatles. It resembled his dorm room; maybe not as much had changed as I'd originally thought.

At the Strand, I went to the contemporary romance section in the back of the store. Romance novels were my guilty pleasure. I found a book called

The Napper

A Winter In New York by Josie Silver; it seemed like it'd adequately fulfill that particular need for lowbrow art. To balance things out, I picked up *The Bell Jar* by Sylvia Plath. I wondered if my contrasting tastes in literature reflected some kind of double personality–there was the Thuy who liked Pop-Tarts and the Thuy who liked fine cuisine.

When I met up with Oscar by the cash register, he showed me what he'd picked out: *Wolf Hall* by Hilary Mantel and *Breasts and Eggs* by Mieko Kawakami. As we left the Strand, Oscar asked, "What should we do now?" and I snapped, "I need to eat."

"Oh, okay."

We went to a place in the East Village. I ordered a miso ramen while Oscar got a tantanmen. While we waited for our food, I said, "Sorry for being a hangry bitch."

"It's okay. I should have fed you first thing."

With a belly full of sweet broth and noodles, I said, "Do you know what I wish?"

"What?"

"That I could always live in that dreamscape of Paris."

"You mean back with Richard?"

"No, living by myself. Preferably with you visiting me often. The energy in

Paris made me feel whole. Independent."

"You're independent here, too," he said.

"I know, but I feel like in America, I don't feel as fulfilled as I do in Paris. I feel a bit chained down here. Like a cog in the machine."

"I think it's because you're still in college."

"I don't know. Immigration is giving me a headache. I don't know what I'll do once my student visa runs out."

"You could do more school."

"If you know me at all, you should know that I'm *so* over school."

"Right."

"What if we got married?" he said, laughing. "Would that help you out?" I started laughing, too. "You're funny. I wouldn't want to put you through that."

"Why not? Aren't we friends?"

I knew he was joking, and I didn't want to joke anymore about the sad state of my future, so I told him to be serious.

"I'm sleepy," I told him. "I need to take a nap."

"I thought you'd never say it," he said. He drove us back to his apartment, and I plopped myself down on his bed.

"I'm cold. I need a hug."

"Okay," he said, his voice confident.

I wrapped my arms around his waist. The smell of his cologne was now mixed with his perspiration, and I found it intoxicating.

He turned to kiss me. Our lips touched lingeringly, and then he pulled away.

"Sorry," he said. "I don't know what got into me."

My heart started to race.

"Why did you stop?" I asked him, pulling him towards me.

The moment that we'd kissed, and I'd felt his body heat, I'd known that it was over.

*****

The next day, we had a late brunch at a small French brasserie in the West Village called Buvette Gastrotheque. I ordered a croque madame, and Oscar had the oysters. "What are we going to do?" he asked.

"About what?" I said, taking a bite of my croque madame.

"Well, us," he said matter-of-factly. Seeing him so serious made me feel a bit embarrassed.

"I guess we should just do what we do. You have your life in New York. And

I have three more years in Chapel Hill."

He turned away.

"I mean, I don't think you want to do long distance," I said. "Do you?"

Without answering, he took a diamond ring out of his jacket pocket.

"What the actual fuck?" I practically spit out my cappuccino.

"Listen to me. You need to get away from your mom, that much you've made clear. You need your green card. And this might be the way to do it." I felt my face flush. I didn't know what to say.

"Just say yes. When you graduate, you can come live with me in Brooklyn until you get on your own two feet."

"I feel guilty letting you do so much for me."

"You're the woman that I love, and if this marriage fails, I won't put that on you. I just want you to give this a chance. I think you feel the same way about me that I do about you. It just might take some time." "Well, I think getting married is pragmatic. But I can't say one way or another if I'll feel about you the way you say you feel about me. I just don't know what I feel."

"I know. I know that about you," he said wistfully. I knew that I was hurting him, but I needed to be truthful. That was the least that I could do. "Are you sure you want this? Being married to someone as fickle and selfish as me? What if you meet someone that you love more than me?"

"That's impossible."

On Monday, we went to the courthouse to get our marriage license. We had to show the agent our application, passports, and birth certificates. The lady printed out a sheet we'd need to sign at our wedding ceremony. We stood in line behind other couples waiting for the courthouse wallpaper, where people took photos. When we stepped in, I thought I would feel less emotional since I wasn't "in love" with Oscar. At least I didn't think I was in love with him. But I started to cry happy tears as the camera snapped our photos. Outside of the courthouse, Oscar held me tightly and said, "No matter what happens, I'll be here for you."

"Thank you. I love you."

"I love you too."

Linh Luu

That same night, I flew back to Chapel Hill.